Praise for

ROOKFIELD

"Part mystery, part thriller, part batshit horror show, *Rookfield* reads like a midnight episode of *The Twilight Zone* on steroids." — Philip Fracassi, author of *Beneath a Pale Sky*

"The horror of *Rookfield* is mysterious and nuanced and intricate, until it's not, until it's yawing and snarling, the stuff of nightmares. White remains without question one of my favorite writers working today." —Keith Rosson, author of *Folk Songs for Trauma Surgeons*

"*Rookfield* is fast paced and evocative—a foreboding look back at all our worst fears of the last year. It's impossible to avoid a visceral reaction to White's main character, and strap in for the ride as he keeps pushing to find out just what's wrong in the little town where nothing is as it seems. A fast, enjoyable read." —Laurel Hightower, author of *Crossroads* and *Whispers in the Dark*

"With *Rookfield*, White cleverly corkscrews narrative threads, culminating in a compelling, claustrophobic nest of a novella." —Clint Smith, author of *The Skeleton Melodies*

ROOKFIELD

GORDON B. WHITE

TREPIDATIO
PUBLISHING

ISBN: 978-1-68510-003-2 (sc)
ISBN: 978-1-68510-004-9 (ebook)
Library of Congress Control Number: 2021944414

First printing edition: October 15, 2021
Printed by Trepidatio Publishing in the United States of America.
Cover Layout & Interior Layout: Gordon B. White
Cover Imagery: Plague mask by KMA. img (@kmaimg) | Raven element by Katsuri Roy (@stationery_hoe)| Back Photo by Gabriel (@natural) [all from Unsplash - unsplash.com]
Edited by Sean Leonard | Proofread by Scarlett R. Algee

Trepidatio Publishing, an imprint of JournalStone Publishing
3205 Sassafras Trail
Carbondale, Illinois 62901

Trepidatio books may be ordered through booksellers or by contacting:
Trepidatio | www.trepidatio.com
or
JournalStone | www.journalstone.com

For Casey and Saucy – my forever-pod.

ROOKFIELD

1

Leana had taken their son without his permission, but, in light of the pandemic, Cabot Howard's lawyer told him not to expect a court date before the fall. "Everything's closed unless you kill someone," Manzetti was saying over the handsfree as Cabot piloted his dove white Maserati Ghibli onto the highway and away from the city. "Even then, it probably has to be the right someone. But look—family cases, civil cases—that's all getting pushed for now. It's basically end times, you know?"

The wind whipped through the half-open window as Cabot accelerated down the nearly empty parkway. Five p.m. and it should have been bumper to bumper, but it was a ghost town on the asphalt. He shared the road with only a few fleeing specters floating away from the sheltering city. They weren't like him, though; they weren't on a mission. Cabot pressed the gas down.

"You still there?" Manzetti asked, the signal breaking as it struggled to keep up with Cabot's speed.

"Are you still billing me for this?" Cabot asked.

Manzetti chuckled on the other end, but it sounded far away and tired beneath the flow of air from outside. "I'm serious," Manzetti said. "Besides, she's Porter's mother and she'll say it was for his own good, what with the virus. I'm not saying it's right, Cab, but a court's going to consider her side of it, too. I mean, she even told you where they went, so they aren't exactly hiding."

Rookfield. Six hours from their home in the city and at least thirty miles from anything that could even charitably be called a "city."

Rookfield. One letter away from a name that might have made any kind of sense—a town so backwards they'd somehow lost their "B," as Cabot had teased Leana whenever they'd gone to visit her extended family out there. Cabot had indulged her at first and put on a brave face, but in short order the prospect of future trips became a hard no. After just a handful of the all-day driving hauls, he had said he'd pay for her cousins to take the train down to the city and they could be dazzled by all the lights and the running water. That was snide, sure, but he was even willing to meet halfway in some other quaint town for a holiday, somewhere equally boring but at least picturesque, unlike the thick dark woods of Rookfield. There had been no way he was ever going there again—it didn't matter who was there.

That changed, of course, now that it was their son, Porter. Not for a million bucks would he go back to Rookfield, Cabot had told Leana after the last time and the funeral out there. Not for any money, no. But for his kid?

Cabot looked back to his phone in its holster on the console. The call was still connected, Manzetti on the other end still ticking away his billable hours for providing wise counsel and patient advice. Outside, the highway stretched off flat, but the early summer's clouds were darkening, and Cabot could already feel the ghostly memory of the rolling foothills and the winding forest roads that Rookfield held waiting for him in another six hours. All around him, it seemed like a dark nest of trees lay in wait just over the horizon.

"Manzetti," Cabot said. "I should tell you I'm already on the way out to get him."

"Oh for—" Manzetti's professionalism caught his tongue even as his voice broke into a squawk as the bars of reception dipped. "You don't want to get in trouble out there. Even I"—it dropped—"as renowned and well-liked as I"—it dropped—"help you, you know."

"He's my son," Cabot said. "He needs me."

"Cabot," Manzetti was both yelling and whispering through the crackle. A few words came through, "He...safer...city...back," but whatever meat had connected the bones of those ideas was gobbled up by the disruption.

Cabot laughed. "Oh, don't worry. I'm bringing him back."

The line went silent as Manzetti's connection finally let go and dropped off. Cabot rolled his window the rest of the way down to let the wind run its fingers through his graying hair. It held the far-off smell of rain from somewhere out beyond the black top, and Cabot's soul felt alive to recognize the scent. He leaned his head out and took a deep open-mouthed breath of the liberating air, but the force of it—or maybe a bit of dust, some debris zipping past—hit his throat just wrong and pushed him into a coughing fit.

Gasping and choking, he fought to compose himself, finally getting his involuntary spams under control. Fortunately, despite the vicious attack, it hadn't been enough to make him swerve, and so Cabot Howard drove on towards Rookfield more annoyed than before, but just as undeterred.

2

Cabot had left the city later than he'd wanted, having been held back for one more call that became one more after, and although the governor's shelter-at-home suggestions had thinned commuter traffic, Cabot was feeling worn down well before making it as far towards Rookfield as he'd wanted. Entering enemy territory at night, even if it was just a backwoods town of decided yokels and the odd retired snowbird too old to keep flying south, was contrary to good strategy, so Cabot decided to pull into a roadside diner to get a bite and regroup. He had already partially resigned himself to spending a night on the road, which rendered the immediate delay tolerable if not agreeable.

The place he chose—Gertie's Drop-By—was as much for the convenience as it was for the air of authenticity the rows of long-haul trucks in the lot promised. While the name suggested a number of contradictory experiences, Cabot was willing to be an optimist, at least in this regard. When he was a boy, back in the lean years, his family had eaten in diners like this, and while Cabot did not hold any particular affection for them, he still harbored a certain nostalgia for their ready simplicity. He would have to bring Porter to one like this—perhaps on their way home tomorrow—as part of his much-needed education on how the other half lives.

Cabot's Maserati stuck out like a French-tipped thumb as it took the aisles between the Mack trucks. Even parked in one of the few diminutive spaces up front in the section designated to keep small cars corralled away from the eighteen-wheeled behemoths that quietly waited for their drivers, the gloss and fuss of his white sports car set him further apart. If he couldn't already feel his stomach eating itself, he might have tried somewhere else further down the road, but instead he got out, brushed some invisible dust from the front of his shirt, and headed inside. Just project confidence; that was how it worked in meetings with the heads of industry and that's how it would work in Gertie's Drop-By, too.

It was with a tinge of disappointment, then, that nobody turned around to look at Cabot as he entered. Befitting the huge parking lot and open road, the inside of Gertie's was large enough that even the large men sitting at the counter or in the booths all had their own space to be engrossed in their own thoughts as they steadily munched through their turkey sandwiches and steak-cut fries. It was social distancing of a different kind, and where Cabot had been carrying a small hope in his pocket that he would cause some ripple or maybe be called upon to quietly prove his fortitude by standing up to their hard-eyed scrutiny, instead his entrance was a non-event. The bell ringing above the door was as much background noise as the trucks still rolling by on the freeway or grumbling awake in the lot.

"Anywhere you please," the waitress behind the counter called to Cabot. He chose a booth close to the window looking out at the small car lot, and the vinyl squeaked as he eased himself in. The tabletop had been cleared, but an invisible film was still tacky beneath his palms. He peeled them up and placed them in his lap.

"Hello there." The waitress wasn't quite Cabot's age—still early 30s, he guessed—but she looked tired. Marlene, according to the blocky letters punched into the tape across her name tag. For a moment, Cabot felt a silly little disappointment that it wasn't Gertie herself, but who knew if she was even still alive or, for that matter, if she ever had been?

"How are you this evening?" Marlene asked.

"Good," Cabot answered out of force of habit. Was it really evening? He was possessed of a general sense that it was getting, perhaps even had gotten, darker outside, but not necessarily more so than the gathering clouds would have made it.

While he pondered the passage of time, Marlene slid a laminated menu before him like a placemat and put down a red plastic cup of water and ice cubes that still bore the tooth marks of the machine that had spit them out. "Want to hear the specials?" she asked.

After listening politely, Cabot ordered the only one he could remember—a turkey melt—which didn't really sound special, but he was a guest here and wasn't fit to argue. The day at work and the drive so far had not left him with the executive function necessary to peruse the codex of burgers and platters and salads and sides. He handed the menu back to Marlene, noting the same sticky film on it that also clung to the table, and ordered a Diet Coke, too.

"Is Pepsi okay?" Marlene asked as she ticked his order off on her pad.

"It's not," Cabot said. It came out a bit sharper than he'd expected, but Marlene just shrugged. Some people were evidently just particular like that, her shoulders seemed to say. Instead, Cabot stuck with water and ordered a decaf coffee, too.

In short order Marlene returned balancing a mug, a saucer, and a little serving plate with pink and blue packets arrayed around the tiny buckets of artificial cream. She placed them in front of Cabot and then filled his mug from a carafe with an orange plastic lip.

"If you've got much further to go tonight, you might need something stronger," she said.

Cabot shook his head. "I have enough trouble sleeping as it is."

His cup filled, Marlene stopped and looked at Cabot. "Do you mind if I ask where you're headed?" she finally asked. "I don't see many men like you stopping through."

"Rookfield." The name fell like a stone from his lips.

Marlene scrunched her brows down and tilted her chin up as if looking at a map taped to the window just behind and above Cabot, but then she shook her head. "Not familiar with it," she said.

Cabot gave her some vague directions and distances as well as he could, but he'd always been one for driving based more on muscle memory than exit signs. His explanation didn't take, though, and Marlene politely shrugged. "No surprise I don't know it, I guess," she said. "There's lots of those little towns out there in the reaches—the kind you probably never even drive by, but if you did, you'd never know they were off in the woods, living alone." She turned away and went back to attending to the dwindling number of other patrons.

Left to himself, Cabot took his phone out and was pleased to see it was back to getting two bars of reception. A look at the time, though, soured his mood. After the delay in leaving and even just the minimal traffic, he certainly couldn't hit Rookfield until well after full dark, sometime in the wee hours. That wouldn't work. Sleeping on the road would cost him a day, but there was no choice and so he began searching on his phone for hotels a bit further down. When that came up empty, it was motels. At least four stars on the user reviews. Then three. Then two.

The scrolling was a distraction, though, and soon Cabot was back on the phone's Home screen. He was back looking at the red message indicator over the little phone icon in the tray. He opened it, ignoring all the red bullets showing unheard and unchecked messages from Leana. The only one that mattered was the one right at the top, from two nights ago at 11:32 pm—a missed call from a blocked number and a voicemail from Porter. Thank God he'd bothered to listen, Cabot thought, even as he was already pressing the Play button again.

"Dad?" In the recording, Porter's voice was slightly muffled, but the clarity of the muffle made it sound like a landline. *"I'm scared. I miss Mom. I don't like being here near the woods. All the sounds at night. The people. I want to come—"*

"Porter?" A man's groggy voice on the other end cut the boy off. *"What are you doing up? Give me that."* The sound of a phone being passed, and then a voice Cabot recognized after a few listens through as Leana's cousin, Abel Oberhof. *"Hello? Hello?"* After a pause, he asked Porter, *"Who did you call?"*

Timidly, the boy answered: "My dad."

A long sigh from the man. "I'm sorry, Cabot. The boy's just been having bad dreams. Leana will be—never mind."

"But I want—"

But the phone hung up with an actual, antiquated click before Cabot could hear his son's last words.

～

WITH THE CLATTER of silverware being arrayed before him, Marlene was back and Cabot's fixation on the voicemail was disrupted. Cabot laid his phone off to the sticky table's side as Marlene placed the long-awaited turkey melt down before him. The Gertie's Drop-By special of dry white toast, parched turkey, and rubbery yellow cheese spattered with an anemic gravy like a crime scene made an undeniable impression. Before Cabot could force himself to pick up his silverware, though, Marlene asked him: "Family or a home?"

"I'm sorry?" Cabot was thankful for the excuse to look away from his meal as it rapidly congealed.

"In Brookfield," she said.

"Rookfield."

She nodded. "Right. In Rookfield. Most people—other than the regular types, I mean—who stop by here on their way to the far parts of the state either have family out there or a second home for the holidays and the long weekends."

"Or the plague," he added.

"That, too, I guess. Is that it?"

"No," Cabot said. Why was he going out there? Of course, Porter was out there, his only real blood relation. Leana was out there too, hunkered down with her cousin Abel and his wife, Nonie. That was her family though, and whatever Rookfield might hold for him, a home wasn't it. No, once he got Porter they were heading right back to the city.

"Family," Cabot answered. "My son and his mother."

The exhaustion that had clouded Marlene's eyes faded, burned off by a curious brightness. "How old, if you don't mind my asking?"

"Ten. His name is Porter and—" And what? It felt good to talk about Porter to someone who didn't know him or Cabot. To be able to refer to his son in ways that didn't involve custody splits or arguments over after-school activities or trying to pry out what was going on in all those hours he wasn't there. But Cabot also didn't know what he could say that wasn't those things. Sometimes it seemed like there was nothing else—just endless errors he needed to somehow make right. "And he's a good kid," Cabot continued. "In fact, he called me the other day. Said he can't wait to see me." He needed that much to be true.

"I have two myself," Marlene said. "Dina and Jeff. Twins. Fraternal." She looked around the leftovers sitting around Gertie's Drop-By, as if seeing it clearly without the grit of exhaustion, then trembled a bit. "Do you have any pictures of your son? Mine are on my phone, but we can't have 'em out on shift."

Cabot looked at his phone, stuck to the table off to the side of the turkey melt. He pictured going through the steps: unlocking it; opening the photos; tilting the screen away from Marlene while he swiped through in search of a suitable memory. One where Leana wasn't in the background looking cross or you couldn't tell Porter was looking forward more to getting back to his mother's house than to the rest of the weekend with Cabot. His fingertips turned to lead at the thought and his shoulders drooped beneath the weight.

"Sorry," he lied. "It's a new phone and I haven't set it up yet."

That sent Marlene back to the kitchen, the tired film settling back over her eyes. The rest of Cabot's time in the diner, spent forcing his way through the turkey melt with a fatalistic persistence, was a coolly professional affair. Cabot finished his meal; Marlene cleared his plate; he declined desert; he paid his check.

Cabot gave driving a shot and put the Maserati a few miles closer to Rookfield, but with night indisputably fallen, exhaustion setting in, and the melt sitting poorly, his options were few. Using the phone's waning GPS, he made for the closest motel—stars be damned. By the grace of some power, too, he made the turn off and could just see the motel's gleaming "VACANCY" in the distance before he lost the signal again. It was a night of small comforts.

As Cabot pulled into the boxy building's lot, his dove white Maserati again seemed terribly out of place. A few malingerers on the rails outside the upper rooms, puffing smokes and flicking the butts down to the asphalt below, stared at him as he got out. In the handicap space nearest the office entrance, an obese seagull wrestled with a mostly empty sleeve of fries, desperate to get the last bits wedged into the slits. The seagull had a scruff to it, and the gray spatter of dirty water droplets staining its plumage made it look for all the world as if it, too, had no idea what it was doing here, hundreds of miles from where it belonged. Unlike Cabot, though, the bird didn't seem nearly as perturbed.

The gull let out a great squawk as Cabot passed near it on his way inside to ask about a room. Cabot shied away from the agitated creature, giving it a wide berth. Despite a few gusty beats of its wings, however, it wouldn't be distracted from its greasy prize.

3

Cabot slept bad and the morning was bad. Even two cups of instant coffee, black, in the motel lobby after checkout couldn't get him right. He felt like the disheveled seagull from the night before had beaten its way down his throat and into his stomach, turning around in there trying to make itself comfortable. The turkey melt had done a number going in and coming out, it seemed.

He put his hours on the road though, and eventually the exit signs led Cabot to the Millhaven Extension, and from there he remembered it was northwards to the highway—if you could call two switchback lanes through the overgrown woods a highway—that took him to Rookfield. Although it felt like the end of the earth, even Rookfield had the requisite state DOT signs at its outskirts, welcoming anyone unlucky enough to visit first to Osteloosa County and then to Rookfield itself. The real welcome sign, however, was the one a few miles further, just after the trees thinned out but before the buildings began. It was an old wooden number, wide as the side of a trailer, held up about ten feet in the air on thick poles that must have been carved from the ancient red cedars nearby.

ROOKFIELD was all it said in yellow capitals. No welcome, no population numbers, no "Home of the World-Famous Fuck-all" or "Somebody You Probably Didn't Know Slept Here." It just announced itself like a challenge, although Cabot had no idea who might find this place if they weren't already looking for it, and so perhaps the lack of hospitality was actually intended as a deterrent. Either way, he was there, and he wasn't turning back.

Cabot recalled that the town's little cluster of buildings around the main street was easy enough to find just by following what little blacktop they had, but he couldn't recall which of the knotted gravel paths spreading off from it took him to Leana's cousin's house. He remembered it was a bit of schlep, so he pulled into the first no-name service station he found on the nearest edge of the brusque imitation of a town. His hope was that this place was exactly as small and inbred as it seemed, or at least enough for everyone to know each other and where they lived.

Pulling up to the spot closest to the door into the little quick stop shop, he killed the Maserati's engine and checked the center console for the facemask he kept for when absolutely necessary. It wasn't there. For a moment he wondered where, and then, like a nail, he was pierced by the image of it on his desk at the office, peeled off and discarded after yesterday morning's meeting with a particularly rich hypochondriac who wouldn't even shake hands. He recalled, too, the sour smell of his own breath soaked into it, and despite a small annoyance at not having it, Cabot could breathe a little easier.

It would be all right out here in Rookfield, though. While businesses in the city were dead set on shaming patrons and even just passersby into making the ineffectual gesture, Cabot knew from the news that small towns like these were apt to take wearing a mask as a freedom-hating concession to liberal science mongers. He hadn't worn it at the diner, and nobody said anything to him then. Actually, he only ever wore it in the city because it was usually easier than not, and here that kind of virtue signal may well equate to a loss of face at best, or even an ass kicking at worst. So, confidently bare-faced, Cabot locked the Maserati and pushed open the little mini-mart's door, setting the bell over the door tinkling.

He was a little surprised and not a little disappointed that the inside didn't appear much different than the last gas station he had stopped at a couple of hours back. The inside was a little older, a tad more worn and torn, but it had the same racks of candy and chips, the same refrigerated wall of pop and domestic beers. The dark-haired teenager sitting behind the counter, too, might even be the same, were it not for the slight pallor to her skin. The only real difference—not to downplay it, Cabot thought—was the large stuffed raven perched behind her next to the cigarette display. As Cabot smiled and stepped into the store, the young woman raised a cloth face mask from around her neck, securing it over her mouth and nose before she rose from her seat to greet him.

"Good morning," she said, loud and slow enough to be understood behind the muffle of her mask.

"Hello. I was—" Cabot began, but the girl cut him off.

"Forgot something?" she asked, again deliberately loud.

"What? No. I just got here from—"

The girl coughed behind her mask in an outsized performative throat clearing, then nodded towards the door. Cabot turned and, for the first time, registered the *No Mask, No Entry* sign on the door. From the inside it appeared in reverse, of course, but there was no mistaking what she was saying. A spike of agitation prickled him, but Cabot forced himself to smile even wider. He could use his lack of a mask to his advantage and show her he was no threat. She would be able to see he was a nice guy and, moreover, he'd be on his way in just a minute.

"I'll stay over here," he said, sliding in just far enough to let the door close while raising his hands as if to also show he was unarmed. "Social distancing, okay?"

"Sorry, sir. That's not what the sign says." The girl crossed her arms, unmoved. Behind her, the great dead, dark bird cawed at Cabot in spread-winged silence and stared back at the door. Cabot didn't have to look again. *No Mask, No Entry.*

"I get it," he said, his smile slipping just a millimeter beneath the last couple of days' strain. "I'll just be a second. I just need to ask—"

"Sir." Her tone stopped Cabot cold. It was commanding, even more surprisingly so coming from someone no more than nineteen at the outside. She continued: "I don't make store policy, but on my shift, we follow it."

There was no getting around it. The look on her face, at least the set brow above the mask, made it clear this was not up for debate. Behind her, the glass-eyed raven standing watch over the snuff and filterless display mimicked her impassive stare. With no recourse, Cabot opened the door and stepped outside but didn't let it close all the way. Standing just outside the threshold, door propped open, he pointed at the sign. He would comply with the "no mask, no entry" policy, but he was going to ask his question, and if she wanted him to have to be loud about it, well, he'd make sure she heard it. Cabot was only obligated to follow the letter of the law, not the spirit.

Cabot took a deep breath and was just about to finally yell out the simple question he'd been trying to ask when the girl pointed again to the door's signage. This time, however, to the side opposite the mask warning.

Handwritten and taped at eye level: *Please keep the door shut! You weren't raised in a barn.*

Cabot forcefully obliged, shaking the glass in the frame. "Are you happy?" he screamed from his position just beyond the closed door. The young woman just shrugged, her eyes suggesting that such a reaction would take more than he was capable of offering. Surprisingly winded but undaunted, Cabot caught his breath in shallow sips before trying again in a more measured yell.

"I just wanted to ask," he shouted at the closed door, "do you know where Abel and Nonie Oberhof live?"

"What?" the girl shouted back, muffled by her mask and the glass between them.

"The Oberhofs," Cabot tried again. "Do you know them?"

The girl pointed to her ears and shrugged. The stuffed raven behind her mirrored the gesture.

"The Oberhofs!" Cabot shouted again, any attempt at restraint lost. He grabbed the door handle, knuckles whitening as he tensed to throw it open.

"I know them," a small, high voice said from behind. Cabot froze on the verge of his tantrum and turned.

A tiny bird-child stared up at him and he gasped. But no, not a bird-child. His first impression was wrong. It was a child, yes, but the bird face was a mask. It had no feathers, but as what he was seeing sank in, the shape was unmistakable. Made of oiled pigeon gray leather and with glass eye pieces, the familiar long, beaked nose belonged to a medieval plague doctor mask. He had only ever seen them before in movies or once at an overpriced masquerade party, but there was no mistaking it—a little plague doctor, missing only the cloak and the top hat. Even having placed it, though, as the initial shock diminished a new unease set over him. Out here, in the middle of the morning in the middle of Rookfield in the middle of the twenty-first century, he had the odd feeling that the mask was no more natural on the small child than an actual bird head might have been.

"What?" Cabot asked. He realized now, too, that he couldn't immediately tell if the child was a boy or a girl, dressed as they were in oversized hand-me-downs two sizes too big and at least that many decades out of date. He must have been staring, because the masked face gazing back at him bobbed up and down like a drinking bird.

"I know them," the child repeated. "The Oberhofs."

Cabot nodded slowly in return. He stole a glance back into the store, but the girl behind the counter was busy tidying up and paid no mind to either Cabot or the costumed child.

"I can give you directions, if you want," the kid said. Although the voice was incredibly muffled—the mask lacked the resonance one might have expected from the beak-like protrusion, instead sounding as if it were further stuffed with sound dampening material—Cabot was now ninety percent sure this was a little boy.

"Okay," Cabot said.

"But you have to give me a lift out that way, too," the boy added. "Deal?"

Cabot nodded again, still unmoored by what was going on. He knew, objectively, that picking up strange children in a small town was almost certainly ill-advised, but he didn't know what else to do. Besides, between the dizziness he had been feeling all morning and the utter absurdity of the little plague doctor, he couldn't be completely positive there actually was a strange child asking him for a ride and not just some figment of a fever dream.

"Great," the boy said, his high voice almost a chirp. "These legs weren't built for walking, you know?" He kicked his stubby legs to demonstrate the point, an oversized boot almost flying off. "Just give me a minute, okay?"

With the tinkle of the bell above the door, the masked boy entered the store. Cabot pressed his face to the glass, desperately curious to observe if the girl could also see the little boy and, if so, how she acknowledged the intrusion. To his disappointment, the answers were "yes" and "likely not more than she would any other customer." Although Cabot couldn't hear their conversation through the glass door and the masks they both wore, their body language betrayed a familiarity as the boy stood on his tiptoes and pawed through a plastic tub of disposable lighters until he seemed to find the one he was looking for. Then, lighter in hand, the little boy pointed across to the wall of cigarettes behind the stuffed raven.

Outside, Cabot ground his teeth as he watched the girl slide a pack of Pall Mall Reds across the counter and take a bill from the child. So much for following store policy on her shift.

4

The boy in the bird-shaped mask sat in the Maserati's passenger seat. His feet barely touched the floor, but he kept tapping the still-wrapped Pall Malls against his knee, topside down, packing them again and again. Cabot had put the AC on, but the odd smell of the mask's oiled leather and the stuffy floral cloy of whatever was lodged inside and which oozed out of the stitches was enough for him to forgo the cool and roll down the window. As the boy pointed out the way to go, he rolled the flint in the disposable lighter—it was blue and orange with what appeared to be a cartoon eagle wearing sunglasses on the side—but didn't strike it. If the boy did, Cabot thought, that would be the point at which he'd have to speak up.

The boy—Cabot was sure of at least that much now—directed them through the town's center with a bored air. As they rolled through Rookfield proper at a leisurely twenty-five and passed the hardware shop, the grocer's stand, the green public square, and the town attorney's shingle, Cabot noticed quite a few others out and about. It wasn't nearly the ghost town he'd been imagining, especially after the gas station clerk's seeming bugaboo about social distance, but it still wasn't normal. They passed a number of what could only be families out doing chores or maybe just taking the air, but all with the same strange dynamic. Parents or grandparents—lots of grandparents, actually, and usually just one—all wore cloth or paper face coverings in the familiar bandit-style over just their mouth and nose, strapped around their ears or the top of their heads. Each of the children accompanying them, however, wore one of the long-beaked plague doctor-style masks in the same fashion as the boy knocking the pack of Pall Malls beside Cabot.

Despite the odd uniformity, Cabot could see that the elaborate masks were not identical, as one by one they turned their pointed faces and glass eyes to watch the white Maserati creep down Rookfield's main drag. Beyond his passenger's pigeon-hued garb, there was enough variation in the children's masks—the size; the material; the eyes, especially—that he could tell they hadn't come off an assembly line. Some of them, in fact, appeared to be made of quite vintage materials—one's long nose was a beak tipped with green patinaed copper; another's cowl of mahogany leather was so parched and cracked that the tiny girl wearing it looked like a buzzard as she turned to watch Cabot pass. Despite this attention from the plague doctor children and their muzzled chaperones, however, none of them seemed more than curious to see him. If there was any alarm at seeing one of their own riding with this outsider, none of them betrayed it.

"Keep down this way on Hartland Street," the boy said as they approached the church and its memorial garden. The familiar landmark sent a shiver down Cabot's spine, but he put the thought away. "We're going to turn a bit further on where things spread out," the boy said, bringing Cabot's attention back, "but I'll tell you when its coming."

"Thanks," Cabot said. The silence that quickly settled in the car without at least the excitement of the town's attention was like an itch. It was almost immediately too much to bear. They stopped at the town's one stoplight and time froze.

"So," Cabot broke the tension that perhaps only he felt. "That's a nice plague doctor mask you have. I noticed—"

"It's a bird mask," the boy interrupted him.

"Well, actually," Cabot said, "it's a plague doctor mask. Back in Europe, during the bubonic plague—"

"Well, actually, it's my mask and it's a bird mask," the boy cut him off again. Although still muffled by the leather and whatever sickly-sweet potpourri was stuffed in the hollow tip, the boy's tone had an unmistakable edge. "This is Rookfield. It's a rook. That's a bird."

Cabot gripped the wheel. The light was still red. He was flushed, hot, as he struggled to keep his words in. He just needed to get to Leana's family—his family, to Porter—and then this kid would be out of his life forever. He just needed to keep quiet; but the more he tried to swallow them down, the more the words seemed to stick and tickle in his throat, building in irritation until he had to cough them out.

"Well, no, actually, it's a plague doctor mask." Once the first word came out, Cabot knew the rest were beyond restraint. "I know a lot of times, in simple towns like these, a half-remembered history gets stuck in the backwater. Ideas fester and mutate until some piece of common knowledge that was once crystal clear—like what's a goddam plague doctor mask—gets all mixed up and muddied by local custom and superstition until your grandpas and grandmas are all out pushing their babies around in what they think are bird masks because they live in a town—whose name they also forgot how to spell, by the way—that happens to sound like a bird thanks to a chain of degradation from Brookfield to Rookfield, doctor to crow." Cabot shook his head, the unusually heavy venom from Leana and Porter and the drive and the day so far all sloshing around, spilling out in his diatribe. "Just let me tell you, kid, thinking something is one way doesn't make it so. There are things called facts, and they don't fucking care. Things are what they are, whether you like it or not."

The boy had turned to face Cabot during the tirade, and now his long snout seemed dangerously close. Then the boy laughed, an unexpectedly throaty chuckle that bounced around the hollow head until it seemed almost too deep for his small chest. Cabot almost expected to hear it rattle off into a smoker's wheeze or hacking cough, but the boy just turned to look back out the window, tapping the Pall Malls on his knee and spinning the flint in the cartoon eagle lighter.

"You and your facts," the boy muttered.

Shame, of course, returned to Cabot almost as hot as the embarrassment that filled him as soon as the last of his unwarranted aggression had left him. The light turned green and Cabot began to drive again. A few blocks ahead, the main town seemed to end, opening up into yards and then, he remembered, the fields and woods beyond. Even this brief silence and the motion couldn't press down his embarrassment, and so Cabot couldn't help but speak again.

"Hey, kid," he said, trying to glance over at the boy as they rolled through the intersection. "Hey?"

"Stop," the boy said.

"Maybe we just agree to dis—" The flashing light and mournful whoop of a patrol car's siren swooping up from behind cut Cabot off. He steered to the side of the road, the tan patrol car in tow.

They were still within the confines of what could be called Rookfield's main strip, narrow though it was. A few of the odd passersby in the face coverings and their smaller charges in the bird-shaped masks paused on the other side of the street to stare. Under their big round eyes, the attention somehow turned Cabot—the only normal one here—into a spectacle.

The realization crept up from Cabot's stomach and clung in the back of his throat. This looked bad. He'd been at his wits' end, not thinking clearly, when he'd accepted this kid's offer. And now, here he was, in a fancy car with a small boy—a small boy who was holding cigarettes and a lighter—on his way out of town and into the middle of the woods. Behind them, the patrol car door opened.

5

———

The boy in the bird mask let out a long, dramatic sigh as he unwrapped the cellophane from the Pall Malls and pulled the first bit of foil paper out of the pack. Despite the police presence, Cabot couldn't help but watch as the boy pulled out the first cigarette, flipped it around upside down, and slid it back into place. He then took out a second one and held it to the mask's beak as if inhaling the stale tobacco. He kept it pinched between his fingers even as he closed the pack, and Cabot's blood pressure jumped another few notches.

Behind Cabot's Maserati, a tall man in a beige uniform exited the tan patrol car. Although he was wearing purple nitrile gloves and a heavy, professional grade mask with a filter, as he approached Cabot could see from his eyes and the smooth forehead beneath his crew cut that the man was young. Mid-20s maybe; large, but his slow steps made him look nervous despite his badge. Cabot had him pegged right there—this was the one who didn't get away. Here was the small-town boy who never got pushed from the nest and never learned to fly. Cabot could handle this if he didn't make any missteps.

Cabot lowered the power window as the man approached. "Officer," he greeted him.

"Deputy," the man corrected him.

"Deputy," Cabot repeated. He swallowed hard, already on the wrong foot.

"Winslow Everly," the boy in the mask said, shaking his head so the long nose waggled back and forth. "What do you want?" Now it was the deputy's turn to swallow hard beneath his mask, and a little flush crept up his cheek from beneath the covering. Even Cabot felt a tinge of sympathy for this big man if the Rookfield children had such little respect for him.

"I'm just doing my job," Deputy Everly said. "I could ask what you're doing, too." He pointed past Cabot to where the boy held the cigarette between his fingers. "And is that a cigarette? You know you're not supposed to have those. I could call your—"

"Oh, you mind your own business," the boy grunted, but tucked the cigarette away behind his leg. "This man was just giving me a ride out."

As if only just then remembering Cabot sat between them, the deputy squinted down at him. "Is that right, mister?" His intonation trailed off, inviting the blank to be filled in.

"Cabot Howard." Cabot began to lean forward and reach for his wallet. "Do you want to see my license?"

"Nah." The deputy waved the suggestion away like a lazy fly. "What I care about is what exactly brings you to Rookfield today?"

"He's visiting the Oberhofs," the boy offered. "Now would you please let us get on?"

The deputy took a long breath through his mask, the sides sucking in like gills and then puffing back out. "The Oberhofs, huh? And what business do you have with them?"

Cabot's hair prickled and suddenly the air was very clammy. "Family," he said softly.

"Family?" The deputy sounded incredulous. "You have blood in Rookfield?"

How far could Cabot bend the truth, he wondered. Already it seemed too small a community to absorb too many lies, but he had no desire to air his business to the deputy, the boy, or anyone else. Still, it was obvious that there was a right and a wrong answer, so Cabot would have to thread the needle. Coming up wrong might well stick him somewhere painful.

"My wife," Cabot said, although he left out the "ex" part. "It's her family."

"Your wife?" the boy asked.

The previous touch of color drained from Deputy Everly's cheeks. "You mean," he began, but seemed to bite his lip behind the mask. Then he again pointed a damning finger at the masked boy in the passenger seat. "Did you know about this?"

"Of course I didn't." The boy fidgeted in his seat and struggled against the seat belt to turn to face his accuser. "I don't ask everyone who comes into town what they're doing here. He said he knew Abel and Nonie but needed directions. I needed a ride. I didn't do anything wrong."

"You're out here with him now, aren't you?"

"You listen here, Winslow," the boy said, now pointing his own accusing finger back past Cabot, who stared ahead, wide-eyed, as the bickering went on over his lap. "You want someone to interrogate every putz who waltzes into Rookfield, that's your job. What else does Sheriff Arrowroot pay you for?"

The deputy fumed, hands on his hips. He flapped his arms as if to yell or throw his hands up but smothered the gesture and turned around in frustration. After he took a deep breath, his large back heaving up and down, he turned back to the Maserati with his thumbs resting behind his belt and shoulders rounded.

"Fine," Deputy Everly said, once again addressing Cabot. "You can go on, but we're watching you."

"Thank you," Cabot nodded, relieved to finally sense an end to this odd drama for which he'd been more a witness than a participant. "I appreciate that, Officer—Deputy, sorry."

"And you," the deputy said as he looked past Cabot one more time to the boy in the mask. "Make sure he gets there, okay?"

The boy didn't bother to answer, but instead scratched at where the seat belt had rubbed him and looked straight ahead out the windshield. The deputy hung there for a moment, but when it was clear he wasn't going to be dignified with an answer, a little tinge of the embarrassed color returned to the exposed part of his face. He turned to go, but Cabot, having seen the status play by the boy over the deputy, couldn't help trying to get his own last word in.

"Oh, Deputy?" Cabot called, his voice ringing out without the obstruction of a mask. "If my family business with the Oberhofs isn't wrapped up tonight, is there a place around where I might stay the night? An inn or a little B&B, maybe?" He knew there wasn't, but he wanted to highlight, just a little, what the deputy's town was lacking above and beyond the appropriate respect for its visitors.

The deputy, already at his patrol car door, turned but didn't walk back. "Why wouldn't you stay with your wife's family?"

Cabot hadn't expected a retort and when the boy snickered beside him, his cheeks began to burn. "It might be too," he looked for the right word, "uncomfortable, with all of us in just the one little house." Why had he said that?

"All respect due to you, Mister Howard, was it?" the deputy said as he ran his thumb behind his gun belt and stopped at the pistol holstered on his right side, just short of a duelist's pose. For the first time, Cabot noticed the heavy, sheathed hunting knife hanging on the left in counterbalance. "But if your kin don't want you with them, it might be best if you found yourself somewhere else tonight."

With that, Deputy Everly folded himself back into the patrol car, gave one last unnecessary whoop of the siren, pulled out into the road and drove off. Around the streets, the handful of face-covered adults and hideously masked children who had stopped to watch the encounter began to move again. Enjoying the sunshine even as the dark clouds Cabot had outrun on the highway were just now catching up over Rookfield, the citizens resumed their migratory paths around the town.

"Nice guy," Cabot grumbled.

"He's a putz," the boy said. "Now let's get on. I got somewhere to be."

6

Cabot followed the masked boy's directions out of Rookfield's center, the buildings and then houses getting further and further apart, then opening into small clearings hemmed in on every side by thick, untamed trees and forest. Their remaining time together passed mostly in silence, the boy tilting the beak of his mask as he looked at each upcoming intersection. Right. Left. The way didn't look familiar at all, but somehow the turns felt right, the memory of it buried in Cabot's muscles. He probably could do this again by himself, he thought, although once more in reverse to get out was all he ever intended to do.

The Maserati came out of a densely wooded stretch of road and the land opened up around them. A wide, cleared field stretched back to a tree line in the distance, but Cabot hadn't seen this much open space since he'd left the freeway. The only structure around was an enormous box of a building which occupied the part of the field closest to the two-lane blacktop. The size and shape immediately called to mind a decrepit barn, rotted to dark gray and looming back a few dozen yards from the road. The earth from the pavement's edge to the building's front was flat without any lip or gully, and two pickup trucks parked out front showed that the bare dirt had been driven over many times and likely by many wheels.

"See that building?" the boy asked, even though there was no way to miss it. "Let me off up there, then you go down another mile, turn left on Parliament Lane, then the second right, the next left, and you can't miss Abel and Nonie, okay? Don't get lost."

Cabot nodded as he slowed down and pulled over to the shoulder. Closer to the building he could see that it wasn't quite what he had thought. The mottled gray was paint, but the walls looked sturdy. All the panes of glass in the high windows were intact. The massive double door looked solid and well-enforced. A few older men with round bellies and cloth face masks were leaning by a smaller service door, taking puffs off cigarettes they slipped just under the fabric at the far edges of their mouths. Another man sat in a pickup bed, perched on a throne made from tight bales of golden straw. That one slipped the bottom edge of his mask up to pull a sip from a can of Coke, then slid the covering back down. Although they all looked over at the dove white Maserati, none of them moved as the kid in the mask opened the door and hopped out.

"Just remember the directions," the boy said, and repeated them once more, slowly and loudly from behind the absurd mask. "Remember, don't get lost."

In the second-story window of the strange building, a curtain seemed to move. The glossy black material behind the reflective glass quivered as if a watcher had just moved off from the point of observation. Cabot shivered.

"Hey," Cabot called out. "What is this place?"

But the passenger door was already slamming and for a second it seemed to have cut off Cabot's question. Still, the boy must have heard, because—although muffled by the window glass and the plague doctor's beak stuffed with what had to be dried and fragrant flowers—he called back an answer, although one Cabot couldn't quite make fit.

"A playhouse?" Cabot asked himself as he pulled away, leaving the odd boy and the masked men behind forever. Had the boy meant as in a theater, or a place for children? What would either of them be doing out here?

7

Despite being warned against it—twice—Cabot got lost. It was down to Parliament Lane and then left and left, then right, right? Or not, as it turned out. Forty-five minutes on the backroads, trying to let his head, with its muddled recollection of the masked boy's muffled words, duke it out with his gut, which promised it remembered the feel of these roads that he and Leana had last driven years ago, just after Porter was born. Cabot was just about ready to surrender and do something really crazy—close his eyes to shut up his brain, maybe, and let that gut memory steer him there, trees and ravines be damned—when there it was: Leana's Subaru, parked in a driveway just up ahead.

She hadn't let Cabot buy her a new car while they were married, although even after the divorce she did expect him to pay for her monthly parking space. There was something about the old, battered Subaru, though, that must have kept her in touch with where she'd come from, and despite her protestations, she couldn't let go. Where she'd come from wasn't Rookfield, but it was a place as much like it that when they'd first come to visit her cousin Abel and his wife out here, she said it reminded her almost too much of home.

That tie to somewhere else, someplace not the city, even during that time when she had gleefully availed herself of every luxury Cabot had offered, had been part of Leana's allure. Cabot would admit that. That perpetual sense that she wasn't quite a part of the metropolitan world which he'd forced his way into from the outside and had clung to ever since had been electric. Although their pasts couldn't have been further apart, she had reminded him of a part of himself that he'd long ago thought had been swallowed up. While they were together, he could glimpse a reflection of himself that hadn't been throttled by ambition or driven down on the road to success. Why couldn't that life have lasted?

Because that wasn't the full truth, as much as Cabot hated it. Because there was a darker part of him which had felt an immense and selfish joy in commanding Leana's love and attention. He had taken an ever-growing satisfaction in knowing that he, Cabot Howard, had drawn down a wild spirit and, through dint of will, gotten it to give up a little part of its freedom and so he asked for more and more. He became convinced that he possessed a special magnetism which would always hold Leana and that she was the lucky one for it.

He had gotten complacent, though. He had failed to notice that Leana's wild spark never quite went out and, when it flared up after Porter's birth and finally burned a hole through their marriage, the oxygen she drew from their divorce kindled her into a flame he could no longer recognize.

The old Leana would never have brought Porter out here without Cabot's permission. Yet this Leana had and, in a way, Cabot admired the chutzpah it had taken. He honestly thought Leana would have locked herself and Porter away in her apartment, having everything delivered and wiped down with bleach before she let it through the door, boiling her Diet Coke before she drank it to kill the germs. Instead, as the pandemic spread, she'd gone to the parking lot and had the attendants take the Subaru down off the racks. She'd loaded up Porter and driven it all the way out here on her own, out to where it now sat parked beside this squat but sturdy house where Abel and Nonie Oberhof lived. Her whole life—at least her whole life with Cabot—seemed to have been spent running away from a place that he could now see she had secretly wanted to run back to. Well, she'd finally found the courage to do it, or least enough fear to do it, and had taken his son in tow.

Cabot turned into the gravel drive, pulling the Maserati up directly behind Leana's Subaru rather than the stocky Dodge pickup beside it. In part, he wanted to avoid appearing rude by blocking Leana's cousin in, but he'd also like to see her try to run again if she couldn't drive. He got out of the car and approached the house's front porch.

Abel and Nonie Oberhof's house was a single-story box of a building, although the roof was peaked upwards to ward off too much of the winter snow. It sat in one of the historic cleared patches that dotted Rookfield, and the yard around it was neatly kept with a tasteful smatter of decorative shrubs and curated wildflowers. Brick and timber, with a covered front porch, Cabot couldn't place the structure's age, although it hadn't changed in the decade or so since he'd last been here, which spoke well of a simple yet rigorous crafts-manship. Around the house itself, though, to the sides and behind, were the failing rust-roofed lean-tos and gap-ribbed smoker barns that hinted at the farm that once ran here a generation or more back. The only active remains of it were the chickens wandering around the yard and a paddock with a few goats off in the distance. Even the air here had a smell of history: rich earth, the tang of livestock, and some plant with a terrible pollen, Cabot thought. He had been bordering on a wheeze all morning but being out here now was almost too much and he was noticeably short of breath.

Cabot ascended the porch, its sturdy timbers creaking without bowing beneath his step. Before he could open the screen to knock and announce his presence, however, the door to the house behind it opened.

"Abel?" Cabot asked. He was almost certain he recognized the man as Leana's cousin, although his nose and mouth were covered by a cloth face mask stitched from blue-checked gingham. He was older than Cabot remem-bered, of course, his hair now receded up past his crown and gray where it stuck out from the mask's elastic, but he was still a solid, imposing tree of a man. Wearing jeans and a work shirt, he looked every bit the farmer, although he was, Cabot struggled to recall, a veterinarian, maybe? Even though he was pushing, if not a bit past, sixty, it was easy to picture him lifting sheep and calves or holding horses steady under his arm.

Abel nodded. "Cabot." The look on his face showed no surprise at finding his cousin's ex-husband on his doorstep, a day's drive from the city, and having untied the knot of Rookfield's winding roads. If anything, Abel merely looked exhausted, as he pulled the mask inward with his deep inhalation and then puffed it out with a sigh.

"Where's Leana?" Cabot asked as he tried to peer around Abel's bulk in the doorway. He couldn't see up over the man's shoulders, so he tried to lean around. The results were less than illuminating.

"She's here, Cabot, but she's resting." Abel shook his head. "You shouldn't be here."

Cabot was about to answer but then he caught a glimpse of someone in the back. A person—an adult—coming out of the well-lit kitchen and into the dim but cozy living room just beyond Abel. Cabot's pulse quickened. "Is that her?" he demanded.

"Who is it?" the person called. For a moment, Cabot's breath caught at the sight of the straw-colored hair and the sound of a woman's voice, but then the moment was gone. The woman who took shape through the screen's gauze was too stocky, her voice too drawled. Abel's wife, Nonie; Cabot could recognize her now as she drew closer. She, however, was not wearing a mask, and the sight of the first uncovered mouth since he'd eaten at Gertie's Drop-By the day before was momentarily jarring.

"It's Leana's husband," Abel called to her without turning his back on Cabot. After a moment's hesitation, Abel added: "He's just come from the city."

Even from outside, Cabot could see Nonie blanch and throw a fast hand across her nose and mouth. She shuffled backwards into the kitchen, as if afraid to let Cabot out of her sight until she disappeared behind the door frame again.

"Where's Leana?" Cabot asked again, his voice rising. "Her car is outside, so where is she?"

Abel gestured to Cabot to keep calm. "She's resting, I told you."

"And where's Porter?" Cabot stood on his toes, trying to see over Abel's blockade. "Porter!" he yelled into the house. "It's Dad!"

"He can't see you now," Abel said. He shook his balding head and raised his hands as if to show there was nothing he could do. "He's recovering, too."

"You son of a bitch," Cabot growled. "Where's my son? Porter!" Cabot grabbed for the screen door's handle, but Abel struck like a snake, snagging the handle from the inside to keep it closed. A tug of war with Abel would go nowhere, Cabot knew, but he didn't care. He screamed his son's name again and yanked on the handle. Abel was firm and fixed, but Cabot could feel the wood between them beginning to give and he shouted Porter's name once more as he planted his foot on the door frame, ready to yank the screen door off the house if he had to. He gave one final preparatory bellow as a war cry. "Porter!"

"Stop it, Dad! Just stop!"

The shock of hearing his son's voice was so great that not only did Cabot freeze where he was, one foot on the door frame and hands wrapped around the handle, but it took him a moment to realize how muffled the words had been. His son must be wearing a mask.

8

Abel warned Cabot about keeping the proper social distance twice and waited until Cabot had stepped completely off the porch before he opened the door and stood aside. Porter, framed in the doorway like a picture, wore one of the plague doctor bird masks, covered in green velveteen with rose-colored glass eyes and a warm wooden beak. He stepped to the threshold and then, when Abel nodded to him, emerged out into the daylight.

Seeing him, Cabot was immediately struck by how the boy looked different—smaller, in some respect—than the image of Porter in his head. Briefly, Cabot's own ribs felt hollow to think of Porter wasting away, but then immediately they filled with hot anger at how Leana must have let this happen. As the boy moved across the porch, however, Cabot was also struck by how his movements bordered on lively, despite the hesitation. Porter appeared diminished, that wasn't in question, but in another respect, he also struck Cabot as almost more concentrated.

Cabot raised a hand, unsure of where the gesture came from. Like signaling across a battlefield, perhaps. "Hi," he said.

Porter raised a hand in a timid response, but his face was entirely obscured by the beaked mask. The impression was that of a baby bird flapping a single wing, just beginning to test its capacity for flight. "Hi," he replied.

It was definitely Porter's voice, so at least that much was right. There was, of course, a process in the way that fathers and sons talk, Cabot knew. He'd now been on both sides of the divide, and so the tentative starts of "Hi? How are you? Are you eating? Are you sleeping? Was your drive alright?" that he and Porter started with weren't serious topics. They were warm-ups. It was through that slow, inconsequential talk, however, that Cabot coaxed Porter off the porch, backstepping all the while to keep the required distance. Behind Porter, Abel retreated back into the house, only to be replaced by Nonie. Masked with her own gingham face covering to match her husband's, she kept her arms crossed to make it clear she was watching them. Cabot didn't appreciate the implication that he was considered a threat.

"Do you mind if we walk a little?" he asked Nonie as much as Porter, who was now off the steps and in the yard. "It's been a long while on the road and I need to stretch my legs." Without waiting for an answer, he began to amble towards the side of the house, over where the yard opened up to the chicken pen and goats in the distance. He set a general course towards one of the less dilapidated remnants of the prior, proper farm—a fairly sturdy-looking shed —and sauntered towards it, trying to look as aimless as the chickens that wandered the yard, scrounging on the bugs in the grass. Porter slowly followed, and Nonie, frowning and arms still crossed, came down from the porch.

"So really, though," Cabot asked his son as they strolled. "Are you doing okay?"

"Yeah, I'm fine. Uncle Abel and Aunt Nonie have been taking care of me." The boy's long, beaked mask exaggerated his unfortunately typical downcast gaze, transforming him from the usual hangdog into a green-headed grackle looking for a worm.

Cabot had to be careful. "And your mother?"

The long beak turned quickly back to where Nonie had paused beside the rose bushes, then turned back. "Yeah, her, too," Porter muttered.

They were coming up on the open shed that Cabot had been vaguely piloting them towards. Cabot noticed now that it appeared to still contain various tools and implements necessary for rural living, although the rust and rough shape made him hope they were leftovers and not instruments Abel still used in his veterinary trade. An old pick, a wicked hook for hauling sacks of feed, and a pair of heavy iron clippers in a circular cuff, the likely function of which made Cabot shudder. He steered them away, but in that moment when he changed course and the gap between he and Porter narrowed to less than six feet, Cabot dropped his voice low enough to bridge the small distance without Nonie overhearing.

"You called me," Cabot said. For a moment he thought it might have been too low even for Porter to hear, but then his son nodded.

"That's okay," Cabot said, trying to get the words out before Nonie interrupted. "Remember I told you when you and your mom moved out that you could call me any time?"

"Yeah." Porter looked straight ahead, or at least his mask faced that direction.

"And I told you I'd come, right?" Cabot asked.

No answer.

"Right?" Cabot repeated.

"Yeah."

"Well, here I am," Cabot said, and gave a small flourish as if he were a magician who had performed a great feat.

Whatever hope for acknowledgment or applause he had been carrying around, however, fell away into the void of Porter's silence. A nauseous heat rose from his chest up through his neck and burned away his next words. Instead of fulfilling that line, then, Cabot drifted back to six feet apart, feeling Nonie's withering gaze behind him. Father and son ambled on in strained quiet, the scattered chickens following out of a seeming interest in the novelty.

As they turned the corner behind the house and the space opened up to the wide field with the goat pen out back and rows of dark trees standing guard even further than that, Porter finally addressed Cabot: "Why now?"

"Why now what?" Cabot responded.

"Why did you come now? Today?"

Cabot opened his mouth, then closed it. He chose his words carefully, feeling as though this was another needle to thread and that he was dangerously close to being pricked. "I told you. I came because you called me. You sounded scared."

"I know," Porter said. "But why now? Why not before?"

Cabot stopped walking. "Before what?"

"Before I was here. Why not when we were still in the city? Why did you wait until now? Why—" Porter stopped himself, but Cabot could hear the unasked question ringing in the air: *Why did you finally bother this time?*

"Look," Cabot said, trying to see his way through this. "Before—in the city —I knew where you were. I knew you were safe."

"Didn't you want to see me, though?" Porter turned, the mask's wooden beak pointing like a stake at Cabot's chest.

"Of course! But it's complicated. I was busy working, and then there was the sheltering and the distancing." The words felt nakedly disingenuous slipping from his uncovered lips, but now that the torrent had started, Cabot couldn't hold back trying to explain himself to the little plague doctor staring at him.

"Actually," Cabot said, "your mother and I, well, I told you, it's complicated. And I'm not saying it's all her fault—not all of it—but she tends to get really over dramatic, a little crazy even, so when she was calling and calling—"

"Go home!" Porter's screech cut Cabot's ramble off at the knees. For a moment, that same swell of smothering nausea filled his lungs like mucus, but then the sparks of shame and anger touched it and it went up like napalm. It was the masked boy in the car all over again.

"Don't you talk to me like that, you spoiled brat." Cabot jabbed his finger at the green-headed bird mask that stood accusing him. "I drove for two days to come and get you."

Porter shook his head, waggling the mask until it started to slip. "I don't want you here," he said. "You always make things worse. I just want Mom!"

"I think that's enough, Cabot," Nonie called. She had held herself at a safe and respectful distance during the family chat, but now she marched towards them, arms swinging.

"Stop!" Cabot shouted. The unexpected force of it froze Nonie, Porter, and even the chickens scratching at the lawn around them.

"Porter," Cabot calmed his voice. He spoke very even, very slowly: "When you called me, you said you missed your mother."

"Cabot." Nonie took another step.

"Porter, is your mother here?"

The boy's mask swung to Nonie, then back to Cabot. The long nose bobbed up and down as he nodded.

"Porter, don't you lie to me. Is your mother here? At this house?"

Briskly inserting herself between the two, Nonie raised her arms like a wall. "That's enough, Cabot," she said.

Cabot shook his head. "Let him talk, Nonie."

"Your son is tired, Cabot," she said. "Look at him. He's still recovering. Even you can see that."

Suddenly the boy's diminished state made sense. The thin limbs beneath the bird mask, the temerity and, yes, an air of fragility. The revelation punched a hole in Cabot's ribs. "From what?" was all he could manage.

"He was sick when they got here," Nonie said. "Why do you think he's wearing that mask? He's still in a delicate state."

"No," Cabot tried to say, but choked on the denial.

"He had it, Cabot. Leana tried to tell you so many times."

He could picture his phone screen and the red badges showing her attempts. All the missed calls from Leana unreturned, the voicemails unopened, the texts that just said "Please." Every reach rebuffed up until the voicemail she left a week and a half ago where the automatic transcript was so short, he couldn't help but read it: "I'm taking Porter out of the city. We're going to Rookfield." Of course, that one hadn't gotten Cabot here either, if he was being honest; it wasn't until Porter left that message where he sounded so alone. But none of that was Cabot's fault.

"No," Cabot shook his head. "If she had wanted—if she had needed to tell me something like that, she needed to try harder."

"Try harder?" Nonie's voice was burdened by something deeper and sadder than just her anger towards Cabot. With only her mouth and nose covered, the pain she must have felt for her cousin-in-law glittered hard in her eyes. "Do you even hear yourself?"

Porter hid behind Nonie like a baby bird behind the puffed-out chest of a surrogate mother. Behind him, the roaming chickens clucked in mocking laughter as they pecked at the grass. The swell of disgust in Cabot's stomach was getting to be too familiar, too much, and he once again needed to turn away or he would retch it up.

But Cabot didn't turn away. "I'm taking my son back with me, and if Leana wants to stop me, get her out here." He stepped up to Nonie and reached around her to grab Porter even as the boy shrank back. He was in the middle of lunging when Nonie planted herself and gave Cabot a mighty shove backwards.

His feet not yet firmly on the ground when she attacked, Cabot did a shuffle step to try to right himself, but the maneuvering caught an errant chicken that had wandered too close while investigating the kerfuffle. The black and white hen gave a murderously curdled squawk as Cabot's foot came down on it and Cabot went ass over elbows to the dirt. Flapping and squawking, the hen dove back in, hectoring Cabot with furious pecks and dodging his wild swings. The man roared in fury from the ground.

The earth in Rookfield was the kind that seemed to hold water like a grievance, always just below the surface but ready to let it out at the slightest provocation. Cabot's fall had brought it out, and so the damp, dark soil clung to his seat and his knees and his palms as he pushed himself up to standing. He glared at Nonie, whose eyes bulged in evident surprise. Porter cowered.

"Porter," Cabot growled. "You come here right this instant and you take that fucking mask off right—"

The thunderclap of a gunshot stopped him dead. The chickens ran screaming, but the three humans all turned to see Abel standing by the corner of the house, a double-barreled shotgun in his hand. One barrel still oozing smoke, the gun pointed off across the field as Abel surveyed the scene before him. He was still wearing his gingham face covering.

"It's time to leave, Cabot." Abel pointed the gun down at the ground but turned it in Cabot's direction. The still-loaded barrel sat beside its smoking neighbor more like a promise than a threat.

"Where's Leana?" Cabot asked, but the words sounded thin and plaintive, deflated in the face of this challenge.

"She's recovering," Abel said.

"From what?"

"From you," Nonie said.

Cabot turned back to her, ready to shout again, but Porter spoke up from behind her. "It's true, Dad," he said. "She was sick, too, when we got there. She got sick after she saw you last month."

Last month. Last month Cabot had made Leana come out to meet him to sign the last of the papers Manzetti had prepared to wrap up some final and truly picayune arrangements. He could have mailed or even emailed them, but he had wanted to see her in person and talk to her. He'd been carrying one last hope that she'd realize how things weren't as good without him. That she would see she was incomplete, too, or that she needed help with Porter. That he could convince her they could have a new start if she would just give up her odd little prideful experiment.

But Cabot hadn't been sick then. He hadn't. Maybe he had been before—and really, who could tell, when you couldn't get tested—but even if that were true, he had been better by the time they spent that hour or two together signing papers. She'd rushed away so fast, unwilling to stay and talk or even get dinner; they weren't even around each other all that long. Besides, even when he had been sick, it had been mild. If Leana had wasted her time hiding away in her apartment and then running off to her cousin instead of building up her immune system, well, how was that his fault?

"Porter's right," Nonie said. "They were both ill. We're just lucky Porter came back faster."

Cabot shook his head, still refusing to accept the entirety of what he was being told. "I don't care," he said. "You can tell Leana, wherever she is and whatever she's doing, that I'm sorry she got sick. But right now, I'm taking Porter home with me."

"You're not," Abel said. He stepped closer and the gun barrel tipped up ever so slightly. It was not lost on Cabot that the social distance he'd been keeping from the others now made him an easy single target. It had been a way to minimize collateral damage.

Cabot raised his hands in surrender. "You can't keep him here."

"Keep him here?" Abel cocked his head to the side like an owl. "Porter wants to be here."

"He's family," Nonie added, and behind her the boy nodded his long face in agreement.

Cabot should go, he knew that. He should head out and regroup. Marshal his resources and refine his strategy. Call in the cavalry, come back with a plan. The absolute worst course of action would be to antagonize them any further, of course, as he was outnumbered and literally outgunned. Cabot knew all this, but that smug look of triumph on the part of Nonie's broad, flat face that he could see above her mask was just too much.

"He isn't Myrna, you know," Cabot said, and relished the way Nonie's jaw fell open, dragging the mask down beneath her nose. "Taking my son doesn't make up for your dead daughter."

He was going to say something else; he didn't know what, but the venom was flowing, and he was hot and dizzy. The fragility of Nonie's naked nose antagonized him. He was going to say something to twist the knife and really draw the tears. It was about to erupt when the barrel of Abel's shotgun jabbed him in the ribs.

"Time to go," Abel said. "Not one more word."

Abel prodded Cabot back around to the front of the house to where the Maserati sat, its glossy white paint now spotted and brown from rooster tails of mud and dust kicked up along the unpaved roads Cabot had taken to get here. Porter and Nonie followed at a distance, as if they were a strange farewell party which might be unwilling to believe Cabot was gone unless they watched him leave. Despite the armed man, it was those two Cabot couldn't look away from.

The last thing, in fact, Cabot saw as he reversed the Maserati down the drive wasn't the gun Abel kept trained on him, but the way Porter reached out to hug Nonie. That image of the little beaked boy in the green velveteen plague doctor mask with his arms wrapped around the big woman's waist in consolation was the one that stayed burned in his mind. It haunted him all the way back to downtown Rookfield and into the Osteloosa County Sheriff's office.

C abot had expected Sheriff Arrowroot to sit at one of two extremes: the first, a mountain of a man, bursting at the buttons and with three chins beneath a ten-gallon cowboy hat; the second, a long, lean tree root of a fellow, all but baked into bark by the elements save for his drooping silver mustache. Cabot was not expecting Sheriff Julianne Arrowroot, elected five terms running and the last three unopposed. She was his age, maybe, but had kept in much better shape, and the only real sign of her age was the iron gray streak through her dark hair, which she wore pulled back tight. Cabot couldn't see her mouth beneath the heavy-duty respirator mask that he now understood to be department-issued, but from the way she gave him the stink eye from behind her desk, he didn't expect she'd have many smile lines.

Deputy Everly, the one from that morning's traffic stop, stood behind her almost at attention with his hands behind him. Cabot couldn't see his mouth either, but could tell he was grinning. The deputy had been called in as soon as Cabot got into the station and demanded to see someone in charge. Apparently the Osteloosa sheriff was short-handed enough that someone's daughter had been filling in at the desk up front, because when he'd come stomping in the front door, a little girl in a purple suede bird mask and pink cardigan had held up a hand of press-on talons to stop him. She called Deputy Everly and when he saw Cabot, he called the sheriff. Before she would grant him an audience, however, the deputy had not-so-politely insisted Cabot wear the paper surgeon's mask the little bird girl had given him. Sheriff Arrowroot, it had been made clear, would not see Cabot without it.

When Cabot had offered his token protest, the deputy just shrugged. "You want to talk to the sheriff you gotta cover up. We're the big ones here, so we're calling the shots. Don't like it?" The deputy pointed back out the front door.

Despite the trouble Cabot had breathing with the mask on as his hyperventilating rage made it stick and pop from his mouth like a bellows, he acquiesced. With a passable measure of decorum, the deputy then showed him into Sheriff Arrowroot's office. She sat behind an antique mahogany desk —its size and evident craftsmanship at odds with the rest of the mediocre civil service furnishings including an outdated computer, a loudly ticking wall clock, and the scuffed vinyl composite tile floor. The only other personal touch appeared to be the stuffed crow perched on top of the aluminum filing cabinet, but unlike the wide cawing pose of the one Cabot had seen at the gas station, this one stood rigid, head tilted at a sage angle that would make even an owl look foolish. Cabot had hoped that maybe here was someone, finally, who would understand. It would even be worth having capitulated to the deputy, now impossibly smug in his home court, if Cabot could win her over to his side.

It was only twenty minutes later, after telling Sheriff Arrowroot his entire story about Leana and Porter and Abel and Nonie Oberhof and the gun, but receiving only the sheriff's implacable stare over her tented fingertips in return, that Cabot began to suspect it may have been a waste to have compromised his position in an effort to appeal to authority. Things were not going well.

"Now, Mr. Howard, was it?" the sheriff said, only pretending it was a question as she leaned back in her chair. "Having heard your story, and at great length, I must admit I have trouble seeing as to why you are here."

"Here in Osteloosa County, ma'am?" Deputy Everly asked.

"Here in Osteloosa County, yes. Here in Rookfield, too." She spread her hands as if to take in all of her modest domain. "But most of all, Deputy, here in my office."

Cabot grimaced, thankful for once for the face covering. He had parked the Maserati outside in enough of a hurry to straddle two spots, bounded up the short steps with indignant fury, and demanded his audience. Things had clearly gone well-south since then. Nevertheless, recognizing that his apparent righteousness was getting him nowhere, Cabot tried a different course.

"Please, Sheriff," Cabot said. "Please. My son Porter is being held captive."

"By the Oberhofs," Deputy Everly said.

"By his family," the sheriff added.

Cabot bit his tongue, then said, "I'm his family."

"But not the parent with custody?" Sheriff Arrowroot asked, another a false question.

"That'd be the mother," the deputy volunteered. "Mrs. Leana Howard."

"Ah, ah, Deputy." The sheriff wagged a finger to scold him. "That would be the *former* Mrs. Leana Howard. I believe you two are divorced, is that correct, Mr. Howard?"

Cabot nodded.

"Which makes her, once again, Miss Leana Oberhot, does it not?" the sheriff asked.

Cabot didn't respond. His anger couldn't push out through just his eyes, so he began to breathe heavily through his nose again. The paper covering crinkled, keeping time.

"Kin to the same Rookfield Oberhofs who are allegedly holding your son," the sheriff continued. "While his mother is recuperating. With them. In their house." Sheriff Arrowroot opened her hands wide again, then clapped them closed. "Again, Mr. Howard. I have trouble seeing why you are here." She gestured flat-handed to the cloudy gray sky outside the window. "Here." She pointed to the buildings across the street. "Here." She drove her pointer finger into her desk blotter calendar, spearing that day's as of yet X-less square.

Unable to contain it any longer, Cabot shouted. "I told you, I was shot at!"

"You were shot near," the sheriff said and waved it off. "Lots of reasons to shoot at the woods."

"I was forced off the property at gunpoint!"

"Property you were asked to leave," the sheriff said.

"More than once," the deputy added. The sheriff nodded, and the stuffed crow looked down on them all.

"Maybe you should head home, Mr. Howard," the deputy said, bringing his hands back around front and tucking his thumbs behind his belt, sliding them to the sides where gun and hunting knife still hung. "You're starting to sound like you might be unwell." In Cabot's heart, though, beneath his anger and frustration, there was a cold hard certainty. An iron-willed certainty that he couldn't give up now; for Porter's sake, he wouldn't be stonewalled and run off by these rubes.

"No," Cabot said, suddenly forceful and not just furious. The sheriff and deputy exchanged looks. "I told you, they are holding my son prisoner."

The sheriff let out a long sigh. "You have no evidence, Mr. Howard. I know the Oberhofs. Good people. Solid members of the community. They've lost a lot and, frankly, I won't listen to any more baseless attempts to assassinate their good character. Deputy, please." She gestured to Cabot as if to shoo him away.

The familiar frenzy rose in Cabot's chest as the big man approached. He was desperate to take some kind of action, any kind. The boiling venom rose, and he blurted out the first thing that came to mind.

"Leana's kidnapped my son! It's a violation of our custody agreement. She's broken the law and I have connections—my lawyer has connections—and if you two don't do something right now, I'll have the state police and the marshals and the goddam FBI down here turning this backwards town upside down by the end of the day!"

The deputy stopped mid-step, one hand half-reaching towards Cabot. Cabot perched on the edge of his seat. The glass-eyed crow on the filing cabinets stared down with rapt, unblinking interest to see what the next move would be.

10

Deputy Everly, still halfway reaching for Cabot, craned his neck to look to Sheriff Arrowroot. Although her barriers were up and her facade sturdy, the way her eyes narrowed above her mask betrayed her just an inch. Seeing the crack, Cabot's breath came more rapidly. He was on the verge of a victory; he could feel it.

"Perhaps, Mr. Howard," the sheriff measured out her words. "Perhaps we have been remiss in so quickly dismissing your concerns. We don't need other people coming in, stepping all over things as they try to make right what's ours to handle. Wouldn't you agree, Deputy?"

The deputy didn't answer, but he lowered the hand which had lingered outstretched towards Cabot and took a step back.

"Tell me more about what laws your ex-wife has broken, please," the sheriff continued. "And be specific."

But Cabot had exhausted his meagre knowledge instantly as he had spoken. In fact, as the words hung out there now beyond his mask, cooling in the air, he wondered if any of them were actually true. Still, the sheriff's reaction to the threat of outside interference was the closest he'd gotten to any sort of movement. He had to play it out, for Porter.

"I can't explain it fully," he said, quickly adding: "But my lawyer can. If I may?" He pointed to the phone sitting on the edge of the sheriff's desk. Wary, she nodded.

"But mask on," she said. "And dial 9 for an outside line."

Cabot picked up the receiver and dialed Manzetti's direct line. The lawyer's longtime assistant, Emily, put Cabot through.

"Mr. Howard," Manzetti said, his voice booming across the landline. "You're a hard man to get a hold of."

"Sorry," Cabot interrupted him, "but I'm here with the sheriff in Rookfield."

"Oh Jesus, Cab." The stentorian voice cracked. "What did you do?"

"Nothing, honest," Cabot said. "Just let me explain." And so, with Sheriff Arrowroot and Deputy Everly watching—and the sheriff urging him to go faster with the *move it along* hand roll—Cabot quickly brought his lawyer up to speed. The version he provided was, in Cabot's opinion, mostly very accurate.

After he finished, he listened for a minute. "Uh huh," he said into the receiver. "Mmmm. That's what I thought." He took the handset from his ear and held it out to the sheriff. "He wants to talk to you."

Cabot sat back and crossed his arms after Sheriff Arrowroot took the receiver, although she did so with a tissue covering her palm. She wiped down the mouthpiece and earpiece, then held it up slowly. Cabot smirked beneath his mask and wished the sheriff hadn't been wearing hers so that he could enjoy the look on her face when she got what was coming. He tried not to smile too broadly and give away the game.

"Hello, Mister," the sheriff said, and waited. "Mr. Manzetti, yes. This is Sheriff Julianne Arrowroot of Osteloosa County. Yes, that's right, with our main office in the fine town of Rookfield. Now, Mr. Manzetti, I understand you're going to explain the law to me."

The sheriff winked at the deputy, and he mimed a belly laugh in return. Cabot's heart plunged into his intestines.

"Uh huh. Yes. Oh really." The sheriff gave noncommittal interjections as Manzetti presumably rattled off chapter and verse to her. Obviously disinterested, however, she picked at a row of callouses on the inside of her hand, just below the fingers. They were the kind one might get from lifting weights, Cabot thought, or using tools, like a shovel or an ax. Still half-listening, she picked up a letter opener—one with a hawk's head as the handle and the blade its long beak—and set to digging at the dead skin while Cabot and the deputy watched. "Yep. Oh yeah. Of course."

Finally, she put the letter opener down and sat forward in her seat. She swiped the little pile of dead skin from her blotter and onto the floor. "Well, that sure is interesting, Counsellor," she said. "Now, and correct me if I'm wrong, but all of that requires the court to—" A pause. "Yes, exactly. So, I'll tell you what. When Osteloosa County Superior Court opens back up, oh, this autumn, maybe, you go ahead and schedule that. Mhmm. And when the backlog has been cleared and the local business is all taken care of and you do see Judge Lativan, you please do tell her that Julianne says hello and that I look forward to seeing her and Ralph for the Winter Festival." Another pause. "Uh huh. Yes, thank you, too."

Sheriff Arrowroot held the phone receiver back towards Cabot. "He'd like to speak to you again."

"Hello?" Cabot said, already knowing what to expect.

"Well, she's a piece of work," Manzetti sighed. Cabot didn't respond.

"I tried," Manzetti said, "but my advice to you is still to get out of there. You're lucky they're just jerking you around and not doing something worse."

"I can't do that," Cabot said. He looked towards the sheriff and the deputy, but they were having a whispered conversation. The stuffed crow on the filing cabinet was the only one who seemed to notice or care that Cabot was still in the room.

Manzetti sighed again, dragging it out as if to pad the billable hours. "I figured you'd say that," he said. "Tell you what, though, I might have something for you. It probably isn't much, but call me back in twenty, okay?"

"Okay," Cabot said. He was about to hang up when one final thought struck him. "Wait! Manzetti? One more thing." Sheriff Arrowroot and the deputy were looking at him again, so Cabot spoke slowly and very clearly so they could hear every word through the paper mask they had made him wear. "If you don't hear from me by tomorrow, it's because Abel Oberhof or Sheriff Arrowroot or Deputy, wait." Cabot paused and gestured to the deputy to lean closer so he could read his badge again. The deputy obliged. "Everly—Deputy Everly—have murdered me. That's still a crime, at least, even in Rookfield."

The sheriff gave a noncommittal shrug and Deputy Everly took the receiver from Cabot and placed it back in the cradle, ending the call. Cabot stood to leave without waiting for any further dismissal and received no argument. As he walked out of the office, he pulled the paper mask from his face and crumpled it up, letting it fall to the floor nowhere near a trash can. The girl in the purple plague doctor bird mask squawked at him from the reception desk but Cabot didn't care. He pushed the doors open and took a deep breath of the free and angry air as he stepped out into the gray afternoon. He wasn't going to let them tell him what to do; no, he wasn't going to be pushed around by the Osteloosa Sheriff's Office and its petty tyrants with their tin badges.

It wasn't until Cabot got to the bottom of the steps, though, that he saw the orange parking ticket wedged beneath the Maserati's wiper, flapping like a pinned wing in the growing breeze.

11

W ith the Maserati ticketed, Cabot considered his parking paid for the next half hour at least, and so he headed off down the few short blocks towards the main street. There were twenty minutes to kill before he needed to call Manzetti back and, he checked his phone once more to confirm, the reception was still so weak he'd need a landline to do it. Fortunately, if anywhere in America still had hardwired payphones, it would almost certainly be Rookfield.

Rookfield itself wasn't so bad, Cabot thought, as he strolled the paver-laid sidewalk; at least as far as these bumpkin burgs go. Having not been here in so many years, it seemed the town had missed the smear of economic devastation and the resulting exodus that had picked the flesh from so much Americana over the last decade. The storefront windows were all intact and had displays. Nothing was boarded up or burned out. It would be a fine place, all in all, were it not filled with the odd men and women who obsessed over face coverings to the point of making their children run around in these plague doctor masks like totems to ward off the pandemic. The place itself would actually make a lovely ghost town.

Cabot checked his phone again for the time. It was mid-afternoon, and although the dark clouds accumulating in the sky made it look later than it was, it was still early enough for the shops to be open. There was a pharmacist, a small hardware store with an outdoor display of hay forks and hoes, and a grocery store that occupied a sizable corner lot. The grocery store looked comforting enough inside, and so Cabot ducked in to grab a snack to head off the exhausted slump he could feel coming on. It also didn't hurt that this little errand would nibble away some of the time until he could call Manzetti.

As with so many other doors in Rookfield—indeed, perhaps all the doors in town—the shop's entrance bore the familiar *No Mask, No Entry*. Normally Cabot would make an argument out of principle or vote with his feet and his dollars by going to another establishment more in line with his beliefs on freedom, but there was nowhere else to go. Besides, he was bone tired. Obeying the spirit of the law, if still not the letter, he pulled the collar of his shirt up over his nose and mouth in a makeshift covering. Neck craned forward to keep the tension, he entered the store, gave a stilted nod to the older gentleman wearing an actual cloth mask behind the counter, and then —when he was not immediately chased out or chastised—Cabot entered the aisles.

The store was quaint in a way that skirted the rustic. Clean without a fuss. A few other customers with baskets and canvas bags in their hands gave him a look as he passed but had the decorum to turn away. The whole place had a medium feel, fitting for a large establishment stuck in a small town, the kind with a few bins of the more shelf-stable produce—potatoes, onions, garlic— but mostly shelves of dry goods. No pre-made food, Cabot noted with disappointment; no chance for a sandwich or other adequate sustenance. Stomach growling at having been led astray, Cabot picked up a few granola bars and a bag of chips, then directed himself towards the wall of refrigerators in the back for a bottle of water.

On his way, Cabot passed a display stand with few passels of odd potpourri in golf ball-size sachets. They looked handmade, and even through his shirt, the cloying floral smell permeated the air and reminded him of the masked boy who had ridden in his car that morning. He paused, taking another whiff. There was a terrible odor, too. Something like death. He leaned away, the movement of his shoulders pulling the shirt-mask even tighter, but no, the reek was still there. In fact, it was even stronger. It was, Cabot realized with embarrassment, him.

The two days of travel, the cheap motel soaps, and the full day of driving, walking, and sweating aggressively across Rookfield had created a noticeable aroma rising from his skin. The incongruity of his immediate experience—the cozy store, the abundant food and drink, and yet Cabot drowning in his own inescapable stench—was overwhelming. He stole a glance back at the man behind the front counter, but the man had turned away politely and was idly dusting the large stuffed bird behind the counter. So concerned was Cabot with his odor, and particularly whether or not it was noticeable to the handful of other masked shoppers, it took him a moment to connect this store's avian display to the birds at the gas station and on Sheriff Arrowroot's filing cabinet. This one, though, was larger than the others, with its inky chest puffed out and head tilted back in an almost regal pose. With some effort, Cabot broke his gaze away and continued on to the coolers in back.

Finally, with a bottle of water obtained and a conveniently shelved stick of sports deodorant, too, Cabot made his way to the front. There was a short line of two older women with cloth masks, one with a bird-faced grandchild alongside her, but the grocer bagged them up and their transactions were concluded with minimal chat or gossip. The thought crossed Cabot's mind that the perfunctory transactions could be a result of his presence, but by that point, Cabot's distress at having to linger in his own ripeness left very little headspace for much else to occupy.

"Did you find everything you need?" the man asked as Cabot dropped his items onto the counter.

"Yes, thanks," Cabot replied. The older man nodded in approval, evidently as satisfied with the result of his store's organizational efficiency as he was with the knowledge Cabot would soon be out of it. Cabot couldn't blame the man, and for once was glad of Rookfield's slavish devotion to the masks, as at least it meant the grocer hopefully couldn't smell what was wafting up from his armpits. As the grocer punched in prices in an old steel cash register, Cabot let his eyes roam across the display behind the man. His attention settled again on the enormous stuffed bird.

After its size, the next and most immediate thing Cabot noticed was that this bird was wearing a crown. The head had been tilted at the wrong angle to see it before, but up close he could see it—not a tiara or a full royal ensemble with arches and jewels and fur and velvet, but a headpiece more in the shape of a paper crown. The prongs rising from the circlet were irregular, like big triangular teeth, yet someone had clearly taken the time to carve it out of a single piece of ash or some other pale wood. It was like a child's drawing of a crown meticulously brought to life without corrections or adjustments, just an ill-formed fantasy made literal, but to what purpose?

"What's that?" Cabot pointed with his elbow at the bird as he handed over his bills.

"It's a rook, of course," the grocer said. He didn't look up as he made change, but he added: "We are in Rookfield."

With great effort, Cabot suppressed his desire to snap back. He had already put together that at some point in the town's benighted past the obvious name of Brookfield had degraded into Rookfield. In the same simple way, their cultural memory of plague doctors from whichever disease-addled hole their ancestors had left to come to the New World had been passed down like a xerox of a xerox until all the kids were running around in those absurd masks they thought were birds, so, too, had their insular communal mind fixated on the "rook" in Rookfield as a sort of town mascot. The way their ancestral game of telephone had garbled a fairly simple message into the current bird-brained obsession may have been interesting in a pitiable sort of way, but it made talking to them nearly impossible.

"I meant on his head?" Cabot asked.

"Her head." The grocer handed over the paper bag of Cabot's purchases. "It looks like a crown."

Cabot couldn't read the man's muffled tone. Was he mocking him? The pale eyes above the cloth face covering, nestled beneath the bushy brows, were no help.

"Thanks," Cabot grunted and left. Only the bell over the door wished him a good afternoon as he left the store.

Even during just those minutes in the grocery store, the shops around him had begun the process of shutting down. Masked storekeepers were sweeping up. Curtains were drawn and placards flipped to *Sorry We Missed You*, and little lists of hours told Cabot when to try again tomorrow. It couldn't be much past four, but the whole town looked like it had somewhere else to be. Behind Cabot, the grocery store door's heavy lock turned over into place. Although the streets appeared to now be empty, and his earlier wish to enjoy the town without the burden of the townspeople was seemingly granted, he felt the weight of eyes on him. Nothing seemed out of place—no curtains moved; no doors opened a crack—but still Cabot could feel the tension in the air as if the buildings themselves were holding their breath.

It was beginning to mist, and the light precipitation was a welcome coolness on Cabot's forehead and face. The clouds overhead had finally drawn completely together, the sky was a flat dark gray, and he wondered if perhaps Rookfield's sudden shutdown heralded a storm or maybe even a tornado. A tornado wouldn't be so bad, Cabot thought, briefly entertaining the possibility of a whirlwind wiping him and the rest of the town completely away. Only one lingering suspicion kept him from fully embracing the fancy, though: If Rookfield was the real world, what worse Oz might a funnel cloud take him to?

Cabot checked his phone again. It was almost time to call Manzetti.

12
----

ookfield—an apparent holdout to most forms of progress—was bound to have payphones. Cabot had a dim memory from years ago of some next to a storefront down near the town church. He ate his recently purchased snacks as he strolled, taking it easy to allow for digestion, and then rubbed the deodorant on, wedging the stick up under his shirt. The result was not "Sport Fresh," but it took the edge off his stink.

Slowed down for once in the last few days, Cabot could feel how unwell he'd been. The sweating, the flushes of nausea, the shortness of breath. He took another swallow of his bottled water, but it couldn't wash down the scratches in his throat. It must be from that damn mask Osteloosa County's finest had made him wear before granting him an audience with the sheriff. Or maybe it was from all the yelling? The one thing Cabot knew for sure was that it wasn't possible that he was sick again. Wasn't the point of the sickness that it was a one and done kind of thing? What would be the point of suffering through it if it didn't make you stronger or immune?

The church was up ahead. Even its modest steeple towered above the rest of Rookfield's squat architecture. It was one of those ancestral buildings that dated back to the turn of a more God-fearing century, but unlike similar antique buildings in other small towns which are lavished with care and upkeep, the Rookfield church was in deplorable shape. The steep roof sagged, and its shingles were peeling up like stiff wings. The once white paint was weathered yellow and peeling, and the stained glass—while intact—seemed dimmed by cataracts of dust. Even when Cabot and Leana had been here for the memorial service years ago on their last visit, Cabot had been struck by how well maintained the adjoining memorial garden where they placed Myrna's ashes had been in comparison to the musty cathedral's inside.

Myrna Oberhof. God, that was tragic. For a second, a wave of disgust seized Cabot's stomach and climbed hand over fist up to his heart. Why had he thrown that in Abel and Nonie's faces? Myrna had been such a sweet girl.

Cabot could see the payphones a block ahead, still there and as strangely out of step with time as the rest of this town, and so he tried to think of Manzetti, Porter, Leana, anyone else. The memory's pull was magnetic, though. He couldn't help but remember when Leana had dragged them out here for Christmas just after Porter was born. Sitting in Abel and Nonie's living room, the two of them joining Leana in cooing over Porter, the fresh new baby, while Cabot and Myrna were left outside the circle. Somehow, though, they had got to talking.

Myrna was almost sixteen and, like almost all almost sixteen-year-olds, she was counting down the days until she got her license. All she could talk about was cars. For his part, Cabot had just bought the red Saab he'd had before the Maserati, and like all new Saab owners, all he could talk about was his car. Just like that, through that oddly perfect confluence, they'd become fast friends, even if just for the night. Myrna wasn't a gearhead by any stretch and her appreciation for the finer vehicles was, of course, a bit circumscribed by dint of her being trapped in Rookfield, but her sincere yearning for the road—to just move—was a hunger Cabot had felt, too. She was going to be the one to get out of there, he could recognize it in her.

They'd left the others doting on baby Porter and gone out into the driveway to look at the Saab. Cabot was showing off some extra feature or other he could no longer recall, but she had been rapt. He was feeling so magnanimous, that when she asked in complete earnestness if she could drive it when she turned sixteen, and that she would be oh so careful, he had wanted to laugh, but he didn't. Instead he said okay. It was a promise. Next time he and Leana came to visit, he'd let her drive it—as long as she promised to keep it safe. As she hugged him, it felt so good to be able to offer such a simple but sincere moment of kindness. The next time they came to visit. It was a promise.

Three months later, Myrna was dead. A few weeks after her birthday, she had been driving home one evening from a friend's house in the fourth-hand Camry she'd scraped and saved to buy when a twenty-three-year-old from two towns over blew through one of Rookfield's four stop signs. That was it: one moment Myrna was the one was who was going to get away, and the next she was gone.

At the memorial service, several people told Cabot that it had been quick, as if he should take that as a kind of consolation. At least she didn't suffer, was how they put it. But even years later, walking past the church on this gray afternoon on his way to the payphones to call his lawyer, Cabot wasn't sure. Was it really better to have that wick instantly snuffed, rather than letting it burn as long as possible? Even if it was only a minute or even a second, would she have wanted to give that up? Did he?

What Cabot really could not shake, however, and what came rushing back to him as he walked past the disused church and the little white cobblestone path that led to the memorial garden tucked away behind the hedges, where Myrna Oberhof's ashes sat in a little marble cubby behind a plate with her name and the dates of her birth and her death, was how short the dash separating those two days seemed. All around Myrna were other prior residents of Rookfield, their starts and ends separated by almost uniformly long gaps. Seventy, eighty, ninety years. But sprinkled at random across the markers were the short-timers, like Myrna at sixteen. Those who had been cut down by sudden disaster. Even separated by marble shelves, the emptiness behind those particular bronze plaques seemed cavernous. Cabot knew that the grief Abel and Nonie felt that day was unfathomable, but when he imagined his own son, Porter, taken away from him by them, he could hear the echoes of it.

He shook his head to dislodge the morbidity; he was there at the payphones. They were slicked by the gentle mist, but a check of the receiver showed, yes, they still functioned, so he punched in a zero and then Manzetti's number to call collect. Manzetti picked up on the first ring.

"Mr. Howard," Manzetti said, using the faux respectful address.

"Mr. Manzetti," Cabot answered in kind. "Please tell me you have good news."

"Nope. Sorry. In fact, as your lawyer, I again advise you to get in your fancy car and get the hell out of there."

"That's not going to happen."

Manzetti waited, but when it became evident Cabot wasn't going to change no matter how much time his lawyer gave him to reflect, he went on. "Yeah, I figured. So, look, there's nothing I can do from here."

"Then why did you ask me—"

"Hold up," Manzetti interrupted. "I said there's nothing I can do. But it just so happens, I know someone in the area."

"Oh yeah?" Cabot perked up. He gripped the phone tighter, pulling it closer to his ear as if to keep the sparrows that had just landed on the church's fleur-de-lis spear gate from eavesdropping. "Who?"

"When the sheriff mentioned Osteloosa County for the fiftieth time, I had a flash. I remembered some clients of mine—rich old guy and his wife— bought some property out there a couple of years back to build a second home. I helped him with the—"

"Manzetti. Please."

"Sorry, sorry. Anyway, I pulled the file, checked the plats, and bam! Rookfield. Or just outside it anyway."

"Do you have a number?" Cabot asked.

"Just a cell, but the reception doesn't seem great there."

Cabot grunted. "It's not."

Manzetti continued. "But I'll give you his info and you can go look him up, okay? Tell him you're a pal of mine and maybe he can help you out. At the very least, it might give you some time to regroup and maybe a lay of what's what out there."

"That sounds great."

"He's a bit old school—I mean, literally old school, like he uses one of those big metal walkers—but he's a decent guy. He's one of us."

"Thank you," Cabot said. "I really appreciate this."

"Yeah, yeah," Manzetti said. "I'm still billing you for this. Okay, you got a pen ready?"

Cabot looked around, but of course he didn't. The street was dark, the stores all closed and the lone masked straggler in the distance was heading away into the gently misting precipitation. "Yep," he lied. "Go ahead."

"All right. His name is Charles Nicholas and his wife is Nora."

"Huh," Cabot said. "Like the Dashiell Hammet book?"

"What?" Manzetti asked. "Have you suffered a head trauma out there?"

"No, no. *The Thin Man*."

"Like, Slenderman? Listen, don't go getting spooky on me, pal."

"No, he was a detective." Cabot trailed off. The discussion had gotten away from him and was getting foggy. "Anyway, never mind, that was Nick and Nora Charles in the book, I think. Not Charles and Nora Nicholas."

"Uh huh," Manzetti said. Cabot could picture him nodding slowly. "Close but no cigar. Are you ready for the address now, or do you need to, I dunno, grab a snack or something? Maybe get your blood sugar up?"

"No, I'm good," Cabot lied again. He was exhausted and could feel himself swimming, dizzy. He shook his head again to clear it. "Give it to me."

"Okay, does Fall's Crown Drive mean anything to you?" When Cabot didn't answer, Manzetti laughed. "Yeah, I thought not. That's why I looked up directions from downtown Rookfield for you."

The lawyer read them off to Cabot—twice—while Cabot tried desperately to keep them in his head. Finally, the twists and turns seemed to stick.

"Got it," Cabot said. "Thanks again, pal."

The line was quiet, then Manzetti cleared his throat. "Cabot," he said. "I'm asking you one more time, please just come back."

The familiar heat rose in Cabot's chest again. Why couldn't anyone understand this?

"I told you no," Cabot said. "Porter's in danger. He needs his father. He needs me. Hell, I think even Leana needs me. They need—"

"But do they, though? Or do you just need them to need you?"

Cabot didn't answer.

"Would it really be that bad," Manzetti asked, filling the silence, "if they were okay without you? Just for a while."

"Manzetti," Cabot said through clenched teeth. "Franco. Buddy. If I wanted a fucking therapist, I wouldn't have hired a fucking lawyer, okay?"

"Okay, okay," Manzetti sounded weary as he spoke. "It's my duty to offer zealous advocacy and wise counsel, but I can't make you take it."

"No. You can't."

"Just be careful, Cab. Please."

"I will," Cabot said. The tension hung on the line like static. He didn't want to leave it like this. It was a bad goodbye. So, Cabot cleared his throat and said in an exaggerated Western movie drawl, "If I'm not back by tomorrow, send the cavalry."

Manzetti chuckled, but it was faint. He sighed. "Bye, Cab."

"Bye, Frank."

Cabot hung up the phone just as the mist became an actual drizzle, whispering against the leaves of the churchyard's trees. The sparrows on the gate had flown away and, from the thick branches of the trees, two damp crows watched as Cabot hurried off down the street. He hustled down the sidewalk as the droplets grew fatter and softer, making it back to the Maserati just before the first real rain fell.

As he buckled into the driver's seat and looked out the windshield, he saw there was another orange ticket beneath the Maserati's wiper. The collection of them there was like monarch butterflies pinned against the glass. He could get out and collect them, of course, put them in the glove compartment to pay them later. That was one option.

Instead, Cabot reversed out of the sheriff's parking lot, wheels squealing on the wet asphalt. He paused at the stop sign at the end of the block, thinking briefly again of Myrna, then took the first turn he could remember from Manzetti's directions. As he left downtown Rookfield and hit the first backroad, he let the engine roar. With a flip of his wrist, the wipers waved, and the orange slips went flying off into the rain like doves on fire.

13

Half an hour or so later, on foot and coming up to the crest of the steep gravel driveway, Cabot could smell the Nicholas family's house before he got there. The quilt of odors—woodsmoke, burnt plastic, an acrid chemical tinge—were dampened by the rain, but still pungent. When the breeze shifted, it came down the ridge of the drive as Cabot lumbered up. There was another scent on the wind, too, but one he couldn't quite place.

Cabot had left the Maserati parked back down the slope. It had been a winding drive up from Rookfield, here into the foothills, made all the more circuitous by the holes in his memory of Manzetti's directions. It was right on the edge of gloaming when Cabot had finally found the turn off for Fall's Crown Drive. From there the driveway was easy enough to find, but halfway up it, still in the trees, he'd come to a locked gate: *Private Access. Do Not Enter.* At least, Cabot thought, it hadn't said anything about masks.

And so, he'd left the Maserati there on the edge of the driveway and set off on foot. He must have outrun the rain on his drive up, because here it was still just a drizzle, even as it escorted the occasional fat, cold drops, but Cabot had failed to pack any protective covering whatsoever. His shirt stuck to him in patches and the cuffs of his pants grabbed at the growing puddles, wicking the dampness up his legs. An unseasonable chill ran through him, but he could see the crest ahead and the break in the wall of trees at the top. His steps quickened; the breeze changed, swishing through the branches; and then the smell of ruin overwhelmed him.

Step by step, the exposed black ribs of the house came into view over the rise. With each movement forward, a little more was revealed as the naked tips of the charred support columns descended from the thin air towards the earth. Then Cabot reached the top and there was the enormous mound of rubble, heaped on the ground like a shovelful of dead earth thrown down by a giant.

It had been a large house. Out of character with Rookfield, certainly, but very much of the style one of Manzetti's clients might build. Judging from the few remaining upright sections protruding from the fire-blackened spall, it had probably been two stories before the roof collapsed. What must have been the open, high-ceilinged foyer and living area in the middle seemed to be mostly clear—the furnishings ruined but the space itself held open by the great stone fireplace which still leaned unsteadily like a bomb survivor—but the surrounding portions that held the double stories of rooms and stairs were indistinguishable piles. It looked almost like a charred nest, arranged around the empty center.

Out here, in the woods, the house must have lurked like a great monstrosity of architecture, out of step with the world but hidden away. The owners likely relished their isolation, but the distance from town meant it had probably burned to the ground without anyone knowing or, at the very least, able to help. Just a blaze and a collapse here in this little clearing, only to be washed away by the rain. It had probably done so very recently, too, guessing by how the smoke still permeated the air. The reek of it made Cabot wish he had saved the mask from the sheriff's office, or at least thought to bring the deodorant from the car to swipe under his nose.

Like any scene of a sufficiently large tragedy, the burnt wreckage held a magnetic allure. It was as if the enormousness of the destruction had imparted to the ruins an outsized density which drew Cabot towards it. In the charred beams and shingles, he could start to pull out faint silhouettes of domestic remnants. A refrigerator door back there, a lump that must be the couch closer by with its cushions, or maybe throw pillows, in a rotten heap beside it. As he stared, little scraps of color and pattern caught his attention, too, emerging from the gloom like the wings of moths cut from book covers and paintings. It was difficult to get a full breath in the heavy air, but Cabot was transfixed by trying to reconstruct what this life must have been like using only the ashes that were left to guide him. One more step closer to the incline of debris that remained of the outer wall, and a small flash of bright blue and orange colors in smoke-cured grass caught his eye. The pattern seemed familiar, and he walked towards it.

"Excuse me!" A woman's voice sliced through the soft patter of the growing rain and spun Cabot around. At the end of the driveway, a woman in a yellow raincoat with matching boots and a black umbrella stared at him. Despite the weather and her distance from Cabot, she displayed Rookfield's customary over-cautiousness by wearing a very serious mask with a respirator valve over her nose and mouth. "Can I help you?" she asked through the obstruction.

Caught off guard, Cabot's mind blanked. He tried to grasp the names Manzetti had given him. "Mrs. Charles?" it finally came to him. "Nora Charles?"

"Yes?" she asked, approaching slowly. "What are you doing here?"

"I'm sorry," Cabot said. He raised his hands to demonstrate his harmlessness, even as it occurred to him how he must look standing alone by the remnants of her house—rain-bedraggled; coated by two-days of road scruff; and, if how he felt on the inside was at all reflected on the outside, burned hollow by the nastiness he felt. His mere lack of a weapon probably didn't go too far in comforting her.

"I'm a client of Frank Manzetti," Cabot continued, hands still high. "He's a lawyer. Your husband's lawyer."

The woman was moving, drawing closer even as she circled a little towards Cabot's right, so he turned, too, to match her. "I see," she said. "And why did this lawyer send you here?"

Cabot tried to think how best to explain it. He debated trying to explain the story of Porter and Leana and the Oberhofs and the sheriff and Manzetti, but trying to put it all in order made him dizzy. There was some element to it all that was off-kilter, but he was having trouble seeing the pieces all at once, so he decided to try a different tack.

"Manzetti asked me to check up on you and your husband," Cabot lied.

He kept turning a little as the woman continued moving but nodded toward the wet lumps and piles of waste that remained of the home. "It looks like you've had some trouble."

"We're fine," she said. "It was just a terrible accident."

The woman stopped moving and now they both stood parallel to the low row of debris where the front wall had once stood. Cabot lowered his hands, but the tension between them remained as thick as the lingering smell of smoke. He glanced down and noticed that his circling had brought him next to the bit of color he had seen in the grass. It looked like plastic, orange and blue. Curious, he knelt down to pick it up.

"Wait!" the woman shouted, and Cabot stopped, his hand just closed around the object. "Maybe you can help me," the woman said. "I'm sorry, it's just, you know, I don't know you." She tried to smile with her eyes—a strained, forced thing—as Cabot slowly rose. "I'll tell you what," she said. "Let me just call Mr. Mancini—"

"Manzetti."

"Right," she said. "Let me just call him and make sure you're one of us. Okay?" She reached into the pocket of her yellow raincoat.

"Just hold—" Cabot said, but she was already pulling an object out. He flinched, expecting the second gunshot of the day. But no. It was just her cell-phone. She stared at him over her mask.

"I'm sorry, Mrs. Charles," Cabot apologized. "I'm just on edge."

"We all are," she replied as she swiped her cell phone unlocked.

Cabot, shaken, squeezed his hands into fists as if that motion could somehow help him force himself to get a grip. As he did, the piece of plastic he'd picked up from the charred grass dug into his palm. The shape was instantly familiar.

In front of him, the woman was talking on the phone. Cabot was dimly aware of her speaking—"Yes, Mr. Mancini, please. I'll hold."—but his real attention was already on the object in his hand. Cabot knew what he was going to see even as he was uncurling his fingers: a disposable lighter, warped from the heat. An incongruously cheerful design on what was left of the orange and blue wraparound decal. A smiling cartoon eagle in sunglasses. Just like the one the masked boy from the gas station had been playing with.

The one he remembered the boy had sifted through the jar of lighters to find as a replacement for the one in Cabot's hand.

"What is that, Mr. Howard?" the woman called to him.

"Mrs. Charles," Cabot said, all the pieces starting to fall together. "I don't think this was an accident. I think—" And then he also remembered that Nora Charles was the name of the wife in *The Thin Man*. And that there was no cell reception out here. And that he'd never told this woman his name.

14

When Cabot looked up, the woman was staring behind him, and for the second time in as many minutes, he knew exactly what he would see before he looked. This time, though, he didn't wait but charged forward, closing the distance in a bound and crashing into the woman. She shrieked as Cabot tackled her into the damp black mud and char. He rolled over top of the woman, sliding across her slippery yellow raincoat, and struggled behind her. Then he wedged an arm under hers and hoisted the both of them off the ground, holding her in front of him like a shield. Her black umbrella, crushed in the melee, caught a breeze and limped off like a spider in a daze.

Not ten feet from where Cabot had just been standing was another man. At least, Cabot thought it was a man. The person was wearing a rain-slicked green poncho that hung from their massive shoulders to their knees. Instead of a simple face covering, however, the new person wore one of the full plague doctor bird masks. The material was white leather and the eyes silver, but the mask's beak was sutured in a ragged red crosshatch to resemble jagged teeth. The effect was as much a bloody barracuda as a bird.

So captivating was the horrible face that it took Cabot a second to notice the hunting knife in the man's hand. In a flash, he remembered it from the traffic stop, the evil twin to the pistol on the other side of a belt. Its heavy blade now glistening with rain, a constant rivulet led from the poncho to the person's hand to the knife to the ground in one silver thread of menace. Cabot followed the path and noticed the khaki trousers dappling in the rain.

"Deputy Everly?" Cabot asked, more out of confusion than expecting confirmation, but the bird mask nodded.

"Let her go." The deputy's voice was deep and sonorous as it rang through the mask and out from the embroidered fangs.

Cabot shook his head. "This isn't Nora Nicholas."

"No," the deputy said. "Just let her go."

"Who is she then?"

"It doesn't matter." The deputy took a step towards Cabot and his hostage, but Cabot pressed the lighter against the woman's throat, praying that neither of them knew what was in his hand. It must have worked, because the woman squealed, and the big man froze. He roared, "Let her go!"

"Winslow, please," the woman whined. Whoever she was, she had a connection to the deputy. She began to hyperventilate, shaking in Cabot's arms, and he could feel the sobs building up inside of her. So he squeezed her tighter, trying desperately to hold both of them together in order to get through this.

"Where's the real Nora Nicholas?" Cabot yelled, dragging the woman a step backwards with him.

"She's sick," the woman answered unexpectedly. "But we're taking care of her."

The deputy took a tentative step towards them. "That's right," he said. "We're taking care of her. She'll be fine."

Cabot ground the lighter into the woman's neck and she whimpered. The deputy reared back as if to lunge but didn't. Cabot gestured with his chin to the deputy's hunting knife. "Throw that over to me," he said.

"Hell no," the deputy said.

That was fair, Cabot had to admit. "Okay." He thought for a second. "Then just toss it way over that way."

From behind the blank silver goggles of the mask, the deputy stared at Cabot and the woman. Without turning from them, he threw the knife off towards the driveway. It didn't land as far away as Cabot would have liked.

"Your pistol, too," Cabot said. He remembered the man's cocky gunfighter's pose from that morning's traffic stop. "I know you have it."

For a moment the deputy's arms tensed as if he might try a quick draw, but then he slowly reached under his poncho with his right hand. It emerged with the pistol, barrel pointed at the ground, then the woods, then straight up. The deputy flicked his thumb and the pistol's magazine slid out. With a quick lob, he threw the magazine over his shoulder and into the deep grass behind him, but then he gently laid the gun down by his feet.

"Okay?" the deputy asked.

"Okay," Cabot said.

"Now, I'll tell you again: Let her go."

"No," Cabot said. "Now, I'll tell you again."

"Tell him what?" the woman said.

"I meant, ask." Cabot shook his head. Things were getting fuzzy once more. "I'll ask you again, Deputy. Where are the people who owned this house?"

The woman struggled in Cabot's arms. Her wet hair stuck to Cabot's face, tickling against his stubble, and he shook his head to clear it off. She tried to pull away, but Cabot pulled her back and pushed the lighter against her neck even harder.

"Please, Winslow," the woman called to the deputy, her voice cracking as Cabot pressed her still. "Just tell him, please."

Where Cabot's threats had failed, the woman's entreaties clearly swayed the man. His arms went limp and his beak dipped. "Okay," he said. "Okay."

The deputy straightened again, puffing out his chest and fixing the jagged-toothed beak at Cabot. "The woman, I've told you, is fine. She's back down in Rookfield, at the playhouse. She was sick, but we—the town—is taking care of her."

"Sick how?" Cabot asked.

"What do you— Are you serious?" The bird mask glared at Cabot. "There's a goddamn pandemic out there! It's killed too many people out there to count and you, you come into our town and don't even have the decency or common sense to wear—"

Cabot ground the edge of the lighter into the woman's neck again and she yelped. "I didn't drive all the way out here to be lectured by a yokel in a

Chicken Little mask," Cabot growled. "Tell me where the man is. Where's Charles Nicholas?"

The deputy lowered his gaze and droplets flew from the tip of his beak as he shook his head. "I'm sorry, but he couldn't be saved."

"What does that mean, couldn't be saved?"

"Sometimes it doesn't work. Sometimes people—outsiders, mostly—are too resistant to it." The deputy shrugged and a sheet of accumulated rain fell from his poncho. "Sometimes it doesn't take."

Sometimes it didn't take.

Leana.

Porter said she'd been sick. Abel and Nonie insisted that she was recovering. That she'd be fine. That she couldn't or wouldn't talk to Cabot. A dark egg that had been nesting in Cabot's craw ever since he'd left the Oberhof house began to hatch, a deep fear working into his bones. He'd left Leana alone. He'd driven her here, to Rookfield and these loons. Cabot had abandoned the mother of his child to these psychopaths and now Porter was in their grasp, too.

"What do you mean, it didn't take?" The familiar surge of hot nausea swelled up from within again. "Is Charles dead?"

"No," the deputy said, but with Cabot's hand against the woman's neck, he felt her pulse quicken even further and the tendons twist just slightly, as if to glance at the burned-out house. Cabot turned, too, and now, electrified by the current of life and death surging around them like a lightning bolt about to strike, the other scent on the wind announced itself once more. This time he recognized it—burnt flesh.

Senses keyed up, Cabot now noticed, too, the dark shape beside what he thought to be a pile of ruined cushions beside the scorched couch had a different, more distinct shape. He had to get a closer look.

Cabot dragged the woman across the low line that remained of the outer wall, into the rubble of the Nicholas's house. The uneven debris gave way beneath their feet, but Cabot muscled them through it, pulling her towards the heap in the open patch that had once been the high-ceilinged room with the white stone fireplace that still protruded like a giant's stripped femur in the dimming light. The woman was crying full out now and the hulking bird-faced deputy was threading his way between the ruined walls and timbers, too, unwilling to let Cabot and the woman out of his sight, but Cabot didn't care. He could feel a presence closing in, a great sense of darkness emerging from just behind the trees as the night fell and the raptor-like deputy picked over the house's bones.

Then Cabot was in the slight clearing that remained of the once-grand living room. The blaze had scorched the slate floors and rendered down the furniture and any decor, but the chaos of the collapse had left the area mostly clear, ringed as it was by the outer load-bearing walls. Here was an aluminum and glass coffee table, now melted into slag. There was the couch, leather curled by flames. And there, on the floor beside his melted walker, limbs splayed and twisted in agony, was the late Mr. Charles Nicholas.

The woman screamed and struggled with renewed determination, but Cabot constricted her tighter. He looked down at the remains, however, and almost screamed himself.

The fire had charred most of his flesh, leaving part of it as ash but some rendered down into a blackened cake. The smell was unbearable to Cabot's exposed nose, and even the woman seemed to be dry heaving from the odor despite her mask. But it was the bones that truly struck him. Something was wrong with the bones.

The flames must have warped them, Cabot thought. Where they emerged from the baked flesh, they were a smooth and waxy yellow. A few ribs were cracked, though, and the cross-sections looked paper thin, as if the boiling marrow had hollowed them out from the inside. But it was the shape of them: stretched, twisted. Too long in some places, but like bubbled knots in others. And his face? It was like nothing Cabot had ever seen and he stood transfixed.

With a roar the deputy leapt at Cabot and the woman, his poncho flapping as he flew down from a pile of rubble. Cabot twisted at the sound, though, and the brunt of the deputy's dive hit the woman. The force of the impact knocked them all to the ground and into the sharp pieces of wreckage.

Cabot rolled away, groaning, to separate himself from both his shield and his attacker. As he got to his knees, the deputy was already crouching beside the woman, one hand under her arm to lift her. The masked face turned towards Cabot. The blank silver eyes and vicious, bloodied teeth seemed to snarl. Cabot knew he had only one chance and so he grabbed the closest thing at hand.

With a blood-curdling scream, Cabot swung Mr. Charles's charred and greasy bones down onto the deputy and the woman. The husk shattered over them, yellow bone shards and thick sheaths of cooked meat and muddy ash raining down from the blow. The impact drove the deputy down on the woman, and she screamed as the corpse waste covered her face. Then Cabot ran.

He bounded over and through the rubble with no heed paid to the dozens of scrapes and bruises inflicted on his shins. Behind him, Cabot heard the deputy lumbering in the wreckage, but between the shock of the blow and the mask's limited field of vision, it sounded like he couldn't put a foot right. Cabot ran as fast as he could, not even breaking stride when he swooped a hand down to pick up the deputy's hunting knife as he passed where it had landed. Down the gravel drive, Cabot ran, feet sliding in the slurry that the rain was making beneath the rocks, but there was no way he would or even could stop until he caught the locked gate's crossbar dead in the stomach.

Just past the gate, parked next to Cabot's Maserati, was the deputy's patrol car. He and the woman must have come together, Cabot realized, but that was fine, since he probably only had time to slash one set of tires. Throwing his weight behind the deputy's stolen blade, Cabot drove it into the front and back wheels on the driver's side and hoped that was enough.

Still holding the knife, he was about to open the Maserati's door when he remembered the patrol car's radio. At the same time, just at the nearest dip in the drive above him, the deputy's beaked mask appeared. Cabot rushed back and grabbed the patrol car's door and—he thanked his good fortune for once —it was unlocked. Cabot gripped the radio handset's wire and looped it around the knife's blade. He glanced up through the windshield and saw the deputy just cresting the hill, the woman leaning on him for support and still wiping at the burnt bits of Mr. Nicholas stuck to her face. Cabot slipped the blade through the wire, severing it.

He was sliding out of the patrol car when he noticed the photograph tucked up under the strap of the driver's side visor. In it, the deputy— unmasked, smiling—stood with arms around the imposter Nora Nicholas woman from the hill. She held a swaddled infant in her arms, and while Cabot couldn't see its face, he could guess from the blue blanket that it was their son. The portrait's background was the type of inoffensive moiré that one might find at Sears or an even less expensive photo department, if such things still existed. They looked so happy there—so unlike the bird-faced plague monster and the sobbing, coal-streaked woman wailing beside him. Cabot caught a glimpse of himself reflected in the glass of the windshield, faint but visible enough with the darkness outside providing the backdrop. He looked like a monster, too.

But Cabot was a monster with a mission, he thought as he scrambled back to the Maserati and climbed in. He threw the heavy knife into the passenger seat and started the car. The headlights automatically came on, illuminating the deputy and his wife just ahead on the other side of the locked gate. The deputy raised his hand in a gesture that could almost be a greeting.

Perhaps they understood each other better now, Cabot thought. Their struggle in the ashes had shown one other that although they were on opposite sides of the battle today, they were united by the common drive of a man to protect his family. They could be equals, if not friends. Cabot raised his hand from the wheel, too, returning the gesture. Then Cabot realized that the deputy was holding his pistol.

But hadn't he thrown the magazine away? *Oh*, the thought smacked Cabot in the back of the head. There was still a bullet in the chamber.

Cabot gunned the engine and peeled backward, the Maserati fishtailing in the gravel. The deputy's pistol barked, and the windshield cracked, but in all the Maserati's flailing the shot had gone wide. The ragged hole in the windshield glass and its doppelganger in the passenger's side headrest traced the line of Cabot's fate were it not for slipping in dumb luck.

He put the pedal to the floor, flying backwards like a maniac until he hit a patch of the drive wide enough to cut a three-point turn in two. Roaring down the foothill roads in the deepening darkness, Cabot headed back into the rain. The wind whistled through the bullet hole and drops of water flew in like bats as he accelerated. He knew what he had to do and where he had to go.

He had to save Porter. Save Leana, too. He had to get to Abel's and get them out. Unfortunately, his sense of direction was all scrambled here, so he'd have to haul himself back down to Rookfield first and then retrace his previous steps. Cabot leaned on the gas and screamed at the world as the Maserati flew down towards Rookfield like a wounded eagle.

15

The trip down the hill, winding back close enough to the periphery of Rookfield to regain his bearings, had cooled Cabot to a certain, small degree. A sharp wind had howled through the windshield's bullet hole and each pass of the wiper sloshed water in through the gap, but it was time and distance which drove his burning rage down into a smolder. Back to the town with its darkened and curtained windows, skimming the outskirts, rolling with headlights off past the giant black barn of the playhouse where more trucks and now a few cars had gathered since that morning. He hadn't slowed down, but all the motion at least gave Cabot time to think.

He was mostly ready by the time he got to Abel and Nonie's and tore down the driveway. The ground was soaked, but Cabot was ready enough to whip the Maserati into a sideways skid across the gravel and came to rest perpendicular to Leana's Subaru and Abel's pickup, hemming them both in. It was full-on night and the dim porchlight was choked with moths and motes, but Cabot was ready enough to tuck the deputy's hunting knife up behind the loop of his belt, just below the small of his back, before bounding up the front steps. He had not been quite ready enough, however, to get there before Abel opened the front door and made a show of fastening the hook and eye lock of the screen door. That was fine, though; Cabot could let Abel have his illusion of safety.

"Leana. Porter. Now." Cabot said.

"Good god, Cabot." Abel was still wearing the blue gingham mask over his nose and mouth, but now was dressed in slacks and a button-down shirt that could have been his Sunday finest were it not so late at night. He shook his head, the thin white hairs plastered to top of his scalp with pomade. "Look at yourself, man. You shouldn't be here." He muttered again, almost as if to himself. "You shouldn't be here."

"I know what you're doing," Cabot said. "I know what this place—Rook-field—is doing."

"What do you mean?" Abel asked. Behind him, at the far end of the living room, Nonie's head appeared from around the corner of the hallway leading back to the bedrooms. Neither Porter nor Leana was anywhere to be seen in the strange yellow glow of the heavily shaded lamps just inside. Cabot strained to see what lay beyond the screen, but it was almost dimmer inside the house than it was on the porch.

"What do you mean, what Rookfield is doing?" Abel asked again. "You've seen Porter. He's fine and healthy."

"Says you. If he's fine, then why is he wearing that mask?"

Nonie yelled from the shadows, "To keep him from catching it again, you bastard."

The knife tucked behind Cabot's back was heavy. It drew the belt down against his hip bones until the leather was cutting into them like a saddle. The throb and flush in his chest made his skin burn despite the rain. Only the weight of the blade itself remained cool, calling to him to use it.

"Show me his face," Cabot whispered. "Show me he's fine."

"What are you trying to prove, Cabot?" Abel asked. "Do you think we've done something to him? You've seen him; talked to him. Do you think we'd hurt our—"

Cabot hissed and Abel, to his surprise, fell quiet. What Abel said was true. Cabot had talked to Porter just that morning and other than the possible frailty—or more like a shrinking, perhaps—the boy had seemed fine. Except for the mask, that was. His son's face had been hidden behind that mocking image of a beaked plague doctor, the one that had decayed through ignorance and age into the bastardized bird mask that all the Rookfield children seemed to wear. And as Cabot thought of that, a flash of the encounter at the ruins of the Nicholas house came back to him. The body, Charles Nicholas, his skull —his skull had been different.

Sometimes it didn't take, Deputy Everly had said. Cabot didn't know what the "it" Everly had been talking about was, but Mr. Nicholas's body had been mangled worse than by any respiratory infection. Not just the bones in his torso and his limbs, but his skull. It had been stretched out, almost pinched forward. In the moment before the deputy had attacked him, it had seemed to Cabot that the distortion of Mr. Nicholas's skull might have been a result of the fire. Maybe the lack of teeth was because he'd been an old man. But now, cooled down just a little, Cabot could think. The old man's skull, peering out from within the burnt skin, had looked, at least maybe a little, as if it had a beak.

"Porter," Cabot said. "I want to see his face. No mask."

Abel stared at him but didn't shake his head or otherwise exhibit an immediate response. He seemed to mull it over.

"And if you do," Abel said finally, "will you accept that he's fine? That he should be here with us?"

"Abel," Nonie said from behind, an obvious concern seeping into her words, but her husband waved her back.

"Well?" he asked Cabot.

The question burned in Cabot's heart. If they could prove that his son was safe, that he was fine, could Cabot leave him with them? Not forever, of course, but long enough to get out of Rookfield, come up with a better plan, and then come back? Abel and Nonie said Porter had been sick, which Cabot couldn't confirm other than what they'd all told him, but if Porter was fine now? If he was healthy and wasn't—what? Wasn't a bird-faced monster? Good Lord, was that what he was expecting? Had the stress of the last two days and whatever else was going on inside him, burning him up, really have brought him this far from sensibility?

"Okay," Cabot said. "If you show me Porter's face and let me hear him say he's fine, I'll believe it."

Abel gestured behind his back to Nonie. Even through the screen door, her reluctance was evident, but Cabot watched as she retreated back into the recesses of the house. Then, by inches, she returned into the doorway's frame with a small shape by her side. Cabot's pulse quickened. It was Porter and he wasn't wearing any mask. He still looked thinner than when Cabot had last seen him in the city, yes; somehow smaller, it seemed, but visibly intact. Almost perfect. It was his son—the son he knew—not some imposter or, even worse, his boy but twisted.

"Porter!" Cabot called out.

The boy raised his hand. "Hey, Dad."

"Come here! Come let me see you."

"No." Abel stepped back to fill the borders of the screen. "He's healthier now, but still delicate." There was a softening, though, around Abel's eyes, and the edge to his voice lessened just a bit as he leaned close to the screen separating them and whispered through his mask: "Cabot, you look like death. You know you're not well. Please, for the boy's sake."

The deputy's knife called to Cabot, the cool metal a counterpoint to the weight of the heat and nausea filling him. He was about to act when Abel spoke again, his voice still soft.

"I know what it's like to lose a child, Cabot. I would never let anything happen to him."

The words pierced Cabot. His head fell.

"Okay," Cabot said to Abel. He looked past the man, back to Porter, and raised his hand again in the only gesture he could think of. "I'm glad to see you're okay," he called to his son. "If you want, I can leave you here for a bit to get better, to relax out here for a while. Is that what you want?"

The boy looked up at Nonie, who had left a firm hand on his shoulder throughout. To her credit, though, she didn't seem to give him any cues or tell him what to say. Porter turned back to his father, his naked face smooth and innocent in the dim interior light. Behind Cabot, beyond the porchlight, all the darkness of the world around him seemed to hold its breath, even the rain stopping its whisper, as they waited for his answer.

"Yes, please," Porter said. The words snuffed the heat in Cabot's chest. Like a lamp blown out, the wick inside was dead, his head filled with wisps of smoke.

"Okay," was all Cabot could muster.

He hadn't even had a moment to rest with the decision when Abel sighed loudly. "Can you leave now?" Behind him, Nonie was already shuffling Porter back into the house. The sounds of their movement in the shadows hinted at the re-masking that was occurring back there.

Cabot was tired. Two days of constant motion, bleeding now towards a third, and he wanted it over. Hadn't he done enough now? Hadn't he made sure that his son was safe, even if he wasn't with him? Made sure that Porter was on the mend and that he wasn't some kind of monster, however ridiculous that might have seemed? Cabot could rest now, couldn't he?

Almost. The bones resting in the burned-out house on the mountainside seemed to whistle from far away as the wind picked up just off the porch. The looming shapes of Abel in his strangely crisp shirt and Nonie lingering in the hallway hid a hollowness. The bullet-hole path from the Maserati's windshield straight into the wounded passenger seat drew a line through the absence of the one who had been his companion, then his adversary, and now... Now, where was she?

Cabot shook his head. "Leana. I need to see her, too."

16

Abel didn't respond. His face didn't move, at least not the part visible above the blue-checked gingham mouth covering. Off in one of the dilapidated farm outbuildings an owl hooted, the low and plaintive *Who?* underscoring Abel's stone-faced denial. Cabot's head swam and, to steady himself, he put one hand on the doorframe. The other, he was almost surprised to find, went to the knife's handle at the small of his back. He felt it calling.

"Cabot," Abel started.

"No. No more of your lies and evasions."

"I showed you the boy."

Cabot nodded dreamily. "You did. But if you'll show me Porter but not Leana, I have to wonder."

"Wonder what, Cabot? We told you—she's healing."

Cabot shook his head, but the motion made odd shapes shimmer in and out of existence in the dim light beyond the mesh screen. "You said she was recovering before."

"Recovering, healing. What's the difference?" Abel asked.

Cabot didn't respond. "Where is she? I just want to talk."

"She won't talk to you now."

Cabot shook his head again, but the nausea it stirred was too much. The motion aggravated the delicate balance in his chest, and his breaths became short again.

"I want to speak to her."

"Look," Abel's voice was hard. He frowned, his brows sinking into deep furrows. "What if she calls you?"

Cabot pondered this. He leaned his forehead against the screen, but the metal wasn't cool. The warm mesh pressed into his forehead, all the little gridwork digging into his brain, leaving impressions of empty squares. "When?" Cabot muttered. "When will she call?"

"Tomorrow," Abel said.

"Tonight."

"She can't."

Enough, the knife was saying. Enough of this. Cabot shushed it. He was so tired. "She can't?" he asked. "Or she won't?"

"Can't, won't? What's the difference?" Abel said.

It was the wrong answer. The knife rose, smiling, from Cabot's belt loop and cut through the screen like butter. Abel yelped—a strange, high sound to come from his barrel chest—and fell back, missing the slash. With the veil punctured, though, the tear in the screen became a rend and Cabot, still under the momentum of the first chop, pushed and staggered in through the still locked but no longer intact screen door. He was inside.

That swing, though, had taken the wind from him. Nonie was screaming and down the halls he could hear doors slamming. Abel was forgotten for a moment in the confusion, and Cabot turned, trying to deduce where Leana might be and if she was any of the noises in the increasing din. Somewhere, inside of him, a voice said that this was insane, but the fire in his chest had spread to his skull and he aimed to plow headlong into the house and cut out all of its secrets if he had to. He'd find Leana and take her back, and, having come this far, he'd bring Porter back, too. Down the hallway were the bedrooms, Cabot knew, and if Leana was anywhere in the house, she was there. Knife blade out like a compass needle, he spun.

"Leana!" he yelled. "Porter! I'm here! Come out, I'm not going to hurt you."

His arm exploded in pain, right above the wrist, and the knife went bouncing from his grasp across the floor, coming to rest under the plastic-covered couch. With its influence suddenly gone, Cabot stood and gaped at the sight before him. Abel, holding an iron fire poker that had just cracked down on Cabot's forearm, raised it again. But Cabot didn't need the knife. He was the knife.

Cabot threw himself at Abel, catching him before he could swing the poker again. His hands flailed at Abel's mask, pulling it askew as he drove the big man into the wall. Framed pictures crashed to the ground behind them, but Abel landed two heavy punches to Cabot's ribs and the blows set off a spasm of coughs. Cabot was doubled over gasping when Abel brought both hands down like an axe onto his back and drove him to the floor.

Face down, mouth on the ragged carpet, Cabot couldn't breathe. Like a cartoon ending, the world grew dark from the outer edges inward. His body was giving up, he knew, but he struggled against the exhaustion. Up to his elbows, up to his palms, his knees.

"Leana," Cabot gasped between hacking coughs. He felt like he was being waterboarded, but the attack was from inside. "Porter."

There, in the hallway, were the two of them. His son, once again in the green felt plague doctor bird mask like a little familiar next to his mother. The boy had always been something she acted like she'd conjured up on her own and never truly wanted to share with him. Each cough sprayed bright holes across his vision, bubbles of nothing, but Cabot could still see them—except, no. That wasn't Leana. That was Nonie. She'd taken Leana's spot and stolen their son. His son. Stolen his chance of getting Leana back.

With a wordless howl, Cabot threw himself across the floor, towards where his friend the knife gleamed dully beneath the couch. He was reaching for it there in the shadows when Abel's full bulk crashed down on top of him. What little breath he'd had left was crushed from him as the man fell like a mountain and wrestled Cabot back from the brink.

Abel's thick arms slid around Cabot's neck. His chin was cradled in the crook of the big man's elbow as the other arm looped around behind like a scarf. If this was any other situation, the little narrator inside Cabot's head said, you might feel safe.

Cabot, despite himself, couldn't help but picture Abel's ropy arms holding a pure white baby sheep. As he watched this phantasm, though, as it got harder to breathe and the blood in his head seemed to stop moving and then started to scream, Cabot watched with sadness as the sheep's wool turned black. First a small spot on its flank, spreading like ink until the sheep was black, then the air around it was black, and Cabot, too, lost his hold on the world. Everything went black.

17

Leana. The name was burned into his brain as he rose back from the depths. The right side of his face was cool, resting on a smooth surface. Glass. The constant thread of air along his face was like someone leaning over to gently blow across him and, for a moment, with eyes still closed, he pictured Leana with her face just inches away, cooling him, soothing him. Whispering to him to just relax, keep sleeping. But Cabot could also hear windshield wipers moving a slow pulse outside the veil of his closed eyes and, at each little pause in the apex of their journey, a tiny bead of water hit his face. The vision of his ex-wife's face cracked, a spider web of fractures spiraling out from a bullet hole at the center, air and rain penetrating inwards. Even without opening his eyes, Cabot knew that he was in the passenger seat of the Maserati, being steered down through Rookfield.

From that seed of awareness, his senses began to return. He recognized the feel of the seat belt across his chest, but up under his armpit, and he realized the odd configuration was because there was some coarse binding around his wrists, too. The vibration of the road below hummed upwards through the wheels, through the floor, into his feet and up his legs. He could tell they weren't bound, at least. Beyond that, though, touch and sound gave him nothing further. Cabot tried to breathe in deeply, unsure of what smell might tell him but willing to try; however, his lungs still felt like they were being squeezed in a damp fist. The effort of the attempt was excruciating.

His other senses exhausted, it was now or never, so he risked opening the one eye closest to the window. It was drizzling again, and a light fog had settled over the ground. Outside, streets orange from the sodium lamps were empty and the windows of every building dark. The misty, damp streets of Rookfield were running in reverse, back the opposite way he'd come again and again that day. Back towards the far boundary and the big billboard sign he'd seen just that morning, which now felt like a lifetime ago. The fact of the matter was inescapable; Cabot was being taken out.

Still, even with that knowledge, he was having trouble bringing himself fully out of the groggy darkness. It was odd to be in this seat, the inane thought came to him, strapped down on the side without any control over the movement. The bruised, haggard glimpse he caught of his own reflection in the wing mirror looked like a corpse—a miserable object that was much closer than it appeared. It was an uncanny inversion of how things should have turned out.

There was a light rising up behind the Maserati, though, and the piercing illumination in the mirror cut through Cabot's mental fog. Coming behind them was Abel's truck, its lights low but still bright enough to block out his ability to see who all was inside the cab. Curious, Cabot hazarded a quick glance through his left eye, only half-opening it, to see who was driving the car.

Abel. Taken aback, Cabot opened his eyes completely and Abel caught the motion.

"Ah," Abel said, the blue gingham face cover hiding any of his own surprise. "Look, Cabot. We're just taking you to the edge of town. No one's going to hurt you, but it's better for everyone if—"

In a lurch, Cabot threw himself as far towards Abel and the steering wheel as the seat belt would let him. Caught off guard, Abel's foot pressed down on the gas and revved the engine. Cabot jerked the wheel hard and Abel gave a grunt as he tried to pull it straight and then Cabot leaned in and shoved it back towards Abel, and the Maserati—finally given clear direction—dove straight off the road and smashed directly into a wooden pole. The impact blew the airbags.

It took more than a moment for Cabot to pull himself together, but he had been expecting the impact and the adrenaline coursing through him helped. Abel hadn't been so lucky. The driver had twisted wrong as he tried to steer out of the skid, and the impact caught him in a strange position. His right arm hung at the wrong angle and where he lay across the steering column and the deflating airbag, he appeared dented, for lack of a better word. Abel didn't move as Cabot unbuckled his own seatbelt and staggered out. The rough ropes around his wrists had been too thick to tie tightly, and he shucked the restraints off as he took in his surroundings.

Behind him, still on the road and up the slight embankment, Abel's truck stared down at the wreckage, its headlights illuminating the scene. Cabot could see that the Maserati's hood was wrapped around one of the thick supports that held up the *ROOKFIELD* sign that stood at the town's border in lieu of a welcome. The sign tilted at an angle now, but the Maserati's one remaining headlight shone off into the mist, pointing a way into the night and away from the town. It was there for Cabot to take, if he wanted it. He could make a run for it.

But Rookfield had taken his son. It had taken Leana, too. Abel had been driving him out here to kill him and dump both Cabot's body and his car, that much was obvious. Nobody says they aren't going to hurt you unless they are. Cabot wasn't just going to run away after that.

Cabot turned back towards Abel's truck but, as his eyes adjusted to the beams, he could see the cab was empty. Motor running, lights on, but nobody was behind the wheel. He stumbled away from what was left of his own car and the still man draped across the wheel, then headed towards the truck's driver side door. This would be as fine a ride as any back into town, Cabot thought as he grabbed the handle.

It happened in an instant: Cabot threw open the door. He saw the boy in the bird mask slouched down inside. He saw the shotgun pointing at him. Cabot threw himself to the ground and the shotgun bellowed above him, the blast deafening.

No holes, the thought came as an instant relief. No new pains. Not dead.

Cabot scrambled up. The kickback had thrown the small boy across the cab and against the passenger's side door. It must have dazed him, too, because his small fingers were only just now fumbling to break the breach and slide in two new shells. Without hesitating, Cabot leaned in and grabbed the gun barrel with one hand and the boy's leg with the other, then with a single jerk tore them both out of the cab. The shotgun, Cabot held, but the boy tumbled out onto the asphalt, lying there between Cabot and the truck.

For a split second, he thought it might be Porter, that Abel and Nonie had finally turned his son completely against him. But no. The hair was wrong, the size and proportions were wrong—even in Porter's oddly diminished state. This boy in a red leather plague doctor mask like a buzzard's cowl wasn't his son. As the boy climbed to his feet in the grass, Cabot closed the gun, shells in place. He pointed it at the boy. Things had gone far enough.

But even as Cabot held the barrels pointed at the boy in the bird mask, he knew one truth. He couldn't kill the boy. What would he have had to become, to take someone else's son away? Not just to another town, to another family, but to the great darkness beyond? Cabot may not have been a good man, but he was a better man than that.

Instead, he lowered the gun but grabbed the boy by the beak of his mask. Cabot swung him around, away from the truck and towards the side of the road. Then, Cabot raised his foot and, with a mighty stomp, kicked the boy square in the chest, sending him sprawling back off the lip of the embankment and into the mist. The boy gave a single yelp as the mask came off, the beak still clutched in Cabot's hand. Packed inside the elongated snout, dried satchels of fragrant herbs and flowers fell out, shaken loose without the small head to hold them in place.

Cabot tossed the mask and gun both onto the truck's bench seat and climbed in. He was going back.

18

The rain was coming down now as Cabot rolled the truck back through Rookfield. He remembered well enough the path the masked boy with the cigarettes had taken him on that morning and that he'd run again and again, always looping back toward the center to circle Rookfield and find his way back out. It was Cabot's plan to head back to Abel's and take Porter, now that Abel wasn't there to stop him, but as he reached the stretch of road that passed the old black playhouse where he'd dropped the boy off that morning, he slowed. The muddy field out front was packed with vehicles.

A flood light on the outside lit up the makeshift parking lot, and every car and truck in Rookfield seemed to be there. Cabot killed his own lights and crawled by, taking them all in, searching for one in particular. There it was: Leana's Subaru. Then she must be here, too, having either finally emerged from hiding or been let out. Whichever it was, he knew that the farm would be empty and everyone, Porter included, was here.

He pulled in at the far end of the rows and looked at the great dark barn. The enormous double doors were closed, but a boy—teenager, maybe— leaned beside the smaller entrance with his plague doctor mask tipped up on his head, the beak upright like a horn, as he finished a cigarette. The boy flicked the butt out into the puddles and pulled his mask back down, then slipped back inside. The door was left open just enough that Cabot could see the thin ribbon of light in the frame. There was a way in.

The shotgun and the long beaked mask he'd taken off the boy back at the crash site both lay on the seat beside Cabot, calling to him. His hands itched, and he let himself imagine kicking in the door, guns blazing, but with only two shells and seemingly the whole of Rookfield inside—all except Abel and the boy back at the wreck, and Deputy Everly and his wife still walking down from the mountain home—that Second Amendment dream fizzled. Instead, Cabot slipped the bird mask over his face. With the red leather cowl, the drooping beak, and the smoked glass eye lenses, even he couldn't recognize himself as the vulture in the rearview mirror. It would have to be good enough.

Through the rain, across the lot, Cabot slipped in through the door the smoker had left open. If the crowd of cars had suggested all of Rookfield was here in the playhouse, then being inside and seeing the crowd confirmed it. The single open room was cavernous and lit by a few dim bulbs hanging from the rafters, but it was jammed full of women, men, and children. So many children, in fact. More than seemed possible given the comparatively few adults. All these children, too, in the horrible beaked masks were a conspiracy of tiny leather ravens watched over by the handful of adult-sized plague doctor scarecrows. Gone were the regular face coverings over just the nose and mouth; everyone here, Cabot could now see, wore the full-faced, long-nosed regalia.

Without the dried flowers and herbs that had filled the mask when he had stolen it from the boy, Cabot could smell all the bodies packed together over the hay and manure musk of the farmyard. They were clustered around the edges of the walls, leaving the center open, but Cabot could easily see over the small heads. The floor was covered in straw, but in the middle of the room big bales and lumps of it were arranged into a shape he couldn't yet decipher. Cabot stuck to the back of the crowd, maneuvering around the periphery until he could make out that the shape was a circle. It was only when he stood on tiptoes, however, and could see over the lip of straw and into the center of the whorl, that he realized it was meant to be a nest.

In the middle were two eggs; at least, props that had been crafted to represent eggs, because they were on a preposterous scale. If Cabot had been standing in the replica nest, each egg would have stood up past his knees. Whatever play was being put on tonight, the absurdity of it was unfathomable. He would soon find out, though, because evidently the play was beginning as the crowd began to shuffle and move as the actors approached.

In the reshuffling, Cabot turned his attention back to scanning the crowd for any sign of Porter or Leana. He only barely registered as a handful of adults entered the oversized nest, then wrapped the eggs in blankets and carried them out to rest against the wall. Everyone here looked the same with the masks and the few differences in design and material were blurred by the dim light and press of them all together. It was impossible to tell them apart, and so as he was scanning the crowd his attention was arrested by the old woman—the only one in the playhouse not wearing a mask—who was being led into the nest by one of the adults wearing both a golden plague mask and a crisp white top hat. It took a moment, his vision obscured by the smoky glass of his own mask's eyepieces, but as the officiant turned and Cabot could tell it was a woman, he recognized the long ponytail descending from the top hat. That streak of iron gray belonged to Sheriff Arrowroot.

The proceedings were curious beyond measure, but Cabot had his own concerns. He wanted to whisper Porter's name, to see if anyone turned, but the crowd was virtually silent. The only sound was the murmuring of their heavy breaths echoing in the masks and the old woman up front, who had begun to cough and wheeze. She sounded as if she was dying, and Cabot's own throat began to tickle in sympathy, his own lungs filling, and the feverish heat began to rise back up in him. His own labored rasps echoed in the stolen vulture mask's empty beak, his own soured breath pouring out and then flooding back in. It was so hot and stale; he felt so sick and suffocating. An explosion somewhere between a scream and a cough was building in his chest and Cabot didn't know if he'd be able to keep it in.

Then there was a sudden, merciful coolness as the second set of great double doors that reached from floor to ceiling at the far end of the room began to open. Outside, the rain had relaxed to a misting, but a thick, low fog hung across the wide, flat field behind the playhouse and stretched out to the dark row of trees in the distance. All the pointed masks turned to watch the great empty panorama.

In the distance, a shadow in the tree line moved. At first, Cabot thought it was the wind, or a trick of the dim light and the distance. But no, because the crowd murmured in response as some great shape as large as the trees themselves emerged.

A slam from behind the crowd broke the spell as the access door from the lot was kicked open. Cabot and many—but not all—of the others turned towards the intrusion. The voices rose from a murmur to a dull roar. It was Abel.

Abel, still alive but in great pain, leaned heavily on the boy Cabot had kicked in the chest and left behind. The big man was so draped over the child that Cabot couldn't see his face, but he noted that the boy didn't seem to have found another plague doctor mask. A few of the adults in the room, including Sheriff Arrowroot in her golden mask and white hat, were moving toward Abel, taking him from the boy. Abel was sure to blow Cabot's cover, and Cabot thought again about running, leaving it all behind, but then the enormous croaking from the field drew the barn's full attention back to the open doors.

The enormous thing moving across the field was now close enough to take shape. At first, it looked like an enormous plague doctor shuffling through the mist. The long beaked mask, the mirrored eyes, and the huge, battered ivory top hat came into focus as it bobbed towards them. Hunched beneath its cape, the monstrous doctor hopped as it walked towards them, its pale, gloved hands held close to its chest. The sheer size of it overwhelmed Cabot and everything went blank, except for one tiny, burning thought: This wasn't a *playhouse*, he realized with a strangled laugh. It was a *plague house*.

19

W as it a delirium? A fever dream from a swollen brain and a lack of oxygen behind the mask that had finally burned a hole in his mind the shape of a mammoth plague doctor scurrying across the field? Cabot broke his gaze to look around and see if the rest of the crowd saw it as well, or if he alone could perceive this comic terror. He was both relieved and horrified to realize that they, too, were all raptly watching the insane creature approach. As he took in the rest of Rookfield, though, Cabot noticed that Abel was also being assisted into the nest beside the sick old woman. The boy still beside Abel, Cabot now realized as he could see him clearly, was no boy.

The face on the small body was a man's—fifty-five if he was a day. The large nose and ears, the five o'clock shadow, the wrinkles and laugh lines now furrowed in worry for his friend gave it away. Cabot realized, too, that he'd met the man once, long ago at Myrna's memorial—his name was Claude something or other, and he was Abel's neighbor. Back then, though, he had been larger; he'd been Cabot's size. The man wasn't younger now, though. His head wasn't on a boy's body. He was just smaller.

Looking around the room again with fresh eyes, it all fell into place. These dozens and dozens of children around Cabot—their hair was wrong, too gray or too thin. Their proportions weren't right. They moved without the awkwardness of youth. Now looking closely at the ones nearest him, Cabot could see the crow's feet visible just at the edges of masks' lenses. Cabot began to swoon; the lights dipped and he braced for a fall, but it was only the bulbs dimming as the enormous creature entered the plague house and cast them all in shadow.

Up close, with the light blocked by the absurd bulk of the thing, Cabot could see that it wasn't a plague doctor at all. It was a gigantic six-limbed raven. Its long talons dug into the dirt floor as it stepped gingerly into the nest at the room's center. It held its massive wings of oil-black feathers folded down like a cloak, and two scrawny four-fingered hands of pale, naked goose flesh hung limply by its breast. What he had taken for a top hat at a distance was a rough crown of protruding bone, shaped almost like the one he had seen on the taxidermy bird at the grocery. Reality slipped away as the thing turned its head to look over the assembly of Rookfield.

The crowd moved back, pressing against the walls to give the monster room. Cabot, caught in the swell of movement, found himself trapped, and the drowning tightness in his chest swelled in response. Unable to breathe or turn away, he watched as the hideous bird bent over to pick up the old woman with its false hands. She coughed and wheezed, even as it brought her high up above the ground, her orthopedic shoes dangling like little brown seeds from the vines of her legs. Then with one smooth motion the creature's head darted forward, its beak closed around her, and then it raised its head up, undulating as it worked the woman down its gullet, still intact.

The town cheered, the joyful sound echoing in their masks and through their beaks until it sounded like crows cawing. In the roar, Cabot finally let himself cough, the wet rasp of it muted in the crowd. He stopped, though, and watched as the beast bobbed for a moment, squatting and standing, until it gave a curdled groan and, from beneath it, an egg began to emerge. Cabot stared as the huge egg—as big as the others that had been taken away in the beginning, but still pliable and wet—slid from the monster's gaping cloaca.

Two full-sized men rushed from the sidelines with towels, dodging under the giant bird-thing's bulk to quickly swaddle the egg and carry it out from beneath the talons as the creature clawed and circled. The men placed the egg outside the edge of the nest, near the ones that had been taken out earlier that night. And there, next to those older eggs, were Porter and Nonie. They weren't even looking at the bird, but were focused on the egg nearest them, which was trembling as a thin, hairline crack crept down from its crown.

Cabot began to move through the Rookfield residents, pushing and sliding between them, but they were too enraptured with the spectacle as the creature picked up Abel to notice the intrusion. In the shuffle, Cabot managed to get on the same side of the plague house wall as Porter and the egg. The crack was widening now, some living thing inside pushing out, and Cabot knew that he had to get there to save his son before whatever abomination was inside could hatch.

"There he is!" Abel's scream cut through the crowd's reverent muttering like a scythe. Cabot turned to see Abel, held high above the ground in pallid four-fingered hands, pointing directly at him. The collective eyes and beaks of the town turned towards him, too.

Abel shouted again. "There he—" but was cut short as the bird-thing swallowed him down.

And with that, a tiny dozen hands were on Cabot. With his disguise blown, Cabot thrashed back at them, shoving and swinging his way towards Porter. He batted the arms away. One adult grabbed his mask, but Cabot slipped it off and threw a punch at the assailant, spinning their beak around backwards. Although Cabot had size on his side, the sheer numbers held him back. Face exposed, overwhelmed, the heat and the nausea began to swell up inside. He couldn't breathe, and he began to cough again. It came out in big, hacking heaves and, for a second, the crowd paused. Their stark-eyed terror behind the glass lenses was clear: they were afraid of his sickness.

Ahead of Cabot the egg was hatching, big cracks crossing its surface as Porter dug his fingers in to help pry the pieces away. In a frenzy, Cabot began grabbing and smacking at the beaks around him, still wheezing and coughing. His lungs were on fire, but as he ripped off masks to reveal one little old face after another, they recoiled in fright. The tiny barefaced people scurried off and their panic spread. A few of the adults, Sheriff Arrowroot included, were still trying to get to him, but as the sea of dark beaks parted, the flood of child-sized bodies held them at bay.

Only Nonie, still full-sized and in a purple finch mask but nevertheless unmistakable, turned directly to face Cabot. Beside her, the egg had fully opened, and Porter was digging within, the ooze from inside coating his arms like honey in the dim light. Cabot ran forward across the empty floor, but Nonie braced herself. She caught Cabot in a bear hug and squeezed him tight. More hands, rough hands, grabbed him from behind as Sheriff Arrowroot crashed through the sea of cowering Rookfielders to restrain him, too.

Struggling, spitting, Cabot watched as Porter pulled the creature from the egg, but then gasped as it came into the light. It was no bird-monster. No dark beast or twisted absurdity. It was a tiny woman, perfectly proportioned as an adult, but the size of a toddler. Her long auburn curls were slicked down, but as Porter scooped her up in a towel, still dripping with albumen, Cabot saw her face clearly—Leana.

There, in that frozen moment, held up by Nonie and the sheriff, with the fire raging in his lungs and the flock of Rookfield behind him, he was overcome. Despite the monster in the nest beside him, everything faded as Cabot watched the way his son cradled his mother, freshly reborn from the strange egg but glowing in the dim light, radiant with health. He watched the way her tiny arms held Porter's neck and how he supported her. A deep sense of love and longing filled him and called out their names.

His voice broke whatever magic had held them all, though, because as they turned to look at Cabot, eyes wide, all the warmth and love drained from their eyes. Behind Porter's mask and in Leana's naked face, Cabot saw what they truly felt towards him in their unguarded moments. It wasn't anger. It wasn't even hatred. It was fear.

In that moment, it all washed over Cabot and his knees buckled, the sudden slack pulling him from Nonie and the sheriff's grip. They let him fall to the straw-covered floor, hard. As Porter and the doll-sized Leana backed away, Cabot knew that he was consumed by a sickness worse than any fever. Worse than any cough or flu, he carried it around inside him, spreading it like a plague.

Dizzy, breath labored, Cabot began to drag himself across the dirt. Not towards his son and his ex-wife, who now stood sheltered behind Nonie. Not towards the open doors and the cool rain, or the truck and the shotgun, or the open road. Instead, he dragged himself to the bales that marked the edge of the nest and then pulled himself up to tumble over inside. Unable to raise his head, the swelling of so much sickness and disease making it heavier than stone, all he could see before him were the great onyx talons and the fresh leathery egg from which Abel would soon hatch, mended and whole. Smaller, yes, but quickly growing back to a better version of who he had been before Cabot came in and broke everything.

Darkness zippered in from the edges of the world, and Cabot raised a hand, beseeching the great six-limbed raven plague doctor. What it was, he didn't know. What it offered, he could only hope. As the shallow breaths rattled in his throat and he closed his eyes, Cabot prayed for those strange pale hands to pick him up and offer him either a second chance or, if not that, at least the comfort of the end.

EPILOGUE

The sky was blue above the trees as Franklin Manzetti stepped out from the back seat of his hired black Suburban. The Oberhof house, with its white clapboard and the broad fields dotted with picturesque old farm structures and the odd livestock pen out to the tree line, could have been a photo for a Chamber of Commerce brochure. *Welcome to beautiful rustic Rookfield*, it could say. He might have even stopped to savor all the bucolic shit if he hadn't been there on a mission.

His driver, an off-duty police officer who'd worked with him often enough before, waited in the car as Manzetti walked up the driveway. The pickup truck and the Subaru in the drive seemed in order. Cabot's Maserati, Manzetti observed, wasn't here. He ascended the porch and noted that where a screen door might usually be were empty hinges. Manzetti knocked on the door briefly, professionally. There was a noise on the other side; a movement behind the peephole.

"Would you mind putting on a mask?" a woman's voice asked.

"Oh, of course. My apologies." Manzetti reached into his coat's inside pocket and removed one of his masks. His clients often insisted on such measures these days, and he'd learned there's no precaution that's a waste to take. He even had a whole unopened pack of paper ones in his briefcase back in the car. Manzetti slipped his mask over his mouth and the straps behind the ears. Once it was set, the door opened.

"Hello, Mrs. Oberhof?" Manzetti guessed. The sturdy woman with the blue gingham face covering nodded. "It's a pleasure to meet you," he continued. "My name is Franklin Manzetti and I'm a colleague," he paused, "and a friend of Cabot Howard."

"He doesn't have a lot of them, huh?" Nonie asked.

"Colleagues?"

"Friends."

Manzetti tried to smile wide enough for it to show through his face covering. "He has enough," he said. "Enough to be worried about him."

Nonie laughed. "You don't need to be worried about him."

"Oh no?" Manzetti asked. "Because last time I talked to him—just short of a week ago—he seemed worried about you."

"Me?" Nonie put a hand to her chest. "Whatever for?"

Manzetti looked around. He didn't see anyone else. Still, he leaned in close. "Well, just between you and me, he didn't seem well."

Nonie took the hand from her chest and placed it softly on Manzetti's shoulder. "Mr. Manzetti," she said. "I understand your concern. He came by here and, well, the things he was saying."

Manzetti nodded. "So, you can understand why I'm anxious to find him. Not just for his sake," Manzetti hurried to add, "but for everyone." Again, he lowered his voice, "I'm worried he might be a danger, especially to Porter or Leana."

Nonie laughed, hearty and long. Her mask sucked and blew with the effort. "Oh, don't worry about that. In fact, here, look." She pointed and Manzetti turned to see a boy and little girl coming towards him across the fields. Between them, they held a wicker basket loaded down with eggs. Manzetti immediately recognized Porter, even with the cloth mouth and nose covering, but the little girl in the full plague doctor mask was a stranger. Still, Manzetti had seen enough of those odd, long-nosed masks in their brief drive through Rookfield proper not to be taken too aback. In fact, he'd been directed here by a strange teen in a pigeon gray mask who'd been buying a pack of Pall Malls at the town's one service station when they stopped to ask for directions.

"Porter?" Manzetti asked.

The boy nodded. "Hi, Uncle Frank."

Nonie watched them from the doorway as Manzetti raised a hand in greeting, but he didn't break social distance. "Are you okay?" he asked Porter.

Porter nodded. "Yeah."

Manzetti paused. He hadn't seen the boy in a while, but he looked good. Healthy. Well. Maybe even a little bigger than the last time, although with kids, what did you expect?

"Porter, is your dad okay? I talked to him before he came out here and I just wanted to make sure he's all right."

"He's all right," the little girl with Porter said. Her mask was a strange pink leather with green glass eyes, but the long auburn curls that followed out from the back reminded Manzetti of Leana. Some cousin or other relative, most likely.

"Is that right?" Manzetti asked, looking at Porter. The boy nodded.

"Uh huh. He was really sick when he got here," the boy said. "But he's recovering now."

"Can I talk to him?" Manzetti asked. He stole a glance back to the Suburban to make sure his muscle was still there. The driver nodded to him, everything okay.

"I'm sorry," Porter said, "but he and Uncle Abel went on a trip. They can't talk to anybody right now."

"He and Abel?" That was puzzling.

The little girl nodded, and Porter joined in. "Yeah," Porter said. "But they should be back by tomorrow. We'll see if he makes it tonight." He flinched as the little girl pinched his side, but he didn't say anything else.

Manzetti looked around. There was Porter, who seemed to be fine; Nonie Oberhof, stern but not threatening; and the little girl, who he didn't know but was clearly some local relation. If Cabot was in danger, it wasn't from these three. There was no reason to worry here. So Manzetti nodded and smiled, making a point to show it to everyone.

"Okay," he said. "Well, I'll be staying just two towns over, so as soon as Cabot gets back, have him call me, okay?"

Porter nodded, but the girl and Nonie didn't move to indicate yes or no. Placated, if not satisfied, Manzetti was backing away towards the car when the wind shifted, and a plume of blue smoke came reaching around from behind the house like a finger. The acrid scent made him flinch.

"What's that?" Manzetti asked. "Is something on fire?"

"Just the burn pile," the girl said, and Porter nodded.

"That's how it works out here in Rookfield," Nonie added from the porch. "It's the only way to get rid of some things if you can't throw them in the dump."

There was something strange here, but Manzetti couldn't place it well enough to follow up, so he just nodded. "Well, thank you," he said. "Just remember to have Cabot give us a call."

This time Porter and Nonie agreed, although the girl stayed silent. All three of them watched as Manzetti climbed back into the Suburban and the vehicle reversed down the driveway and pulled off into the distance.

As the vehicle disappeared, Porter turned to the little girl and asked, "Mom, do you think Dad will tell them to leave us alone when he gets out?"

"I hope so, sweetie," Leana said, her voice muffled by the pink bird mask. "I really hope it works."

"But what if it doesn't?" Porter asked, his voice trembling. His mother hugged him, quickly and fiercely, pulling him in tight despite the fact that she was smaller than him at the moment.

"Oh hush," Leana whispered, holding Porter close. "I didn't mean that. Of course it'll work."

Behind them, however, Nonie was bringing down another armful of trash, descending the front step. The big woman picked up a can of kerosene from where it sat just off the porch and, swinging it lightly to a tune that only she could hear, headed back around the house to the burn pile. There was always a way to get rid of things out there in Rookfield.

ACKNOWLEDGMENTS

This book was conceived, written, and edited over the summer of 2020 as a way to keep myself somewhat together for at least a couple of months during the pandemic. Like most people, having my elaborate web of coping mechanisms torn away all at once was a system shock. Throwing myself into *Rookfield* was one step towards wrestling back a sense of normalcy in a very not normal time by channeling just a smidge of that anxiety into something manageable and controllable—well, for a while, at least.

Anyway, on to the woefully incomplete list of thanks...

First, it's not an exaggeration to say I probably wouldn't be here without my wife, Casey, and our pup, Saucy. I can never thank them enough for their love, but I'll keep trying.

Next, I owe my deepest thanks to Rebecca J. Allred. Our electronic spitball sessions and her delightful cartoon "Plagues" gave me the first glimpses of the thing lurking outside the Rookfield plague house.

I'm also so grateful for the people who did the hard work to keep our writing communities together, even when we were literally kept apart, including my Clarion West Class of 2017 cohort. A special shoutout, too, to Molly Tanzer for her Herculean efforts in organizing and leading book discussions / venting sessions that helped her friends out in so, so many ways.

While *Rookfield* was drafted and edited largely in solitude, I'm humbled by my phenomenal friends, colleagues, and role models who agreed to read the finished book and provide their kind words here: Philip Fracassi, Clint Smith, Keith Rosson, and Laurel Hightower.

It also took a village to bring *my* village of Rookfield to life, so my sincere thanks to my publisher, Christopher C. Payne; my editor, Scarlett R. Algee; and my proofreader, Sean Leonard.

Double-thanks to Scarlett, too, for letting me burn off some extra lockdown energy by doing the cover. My thanks to Vina Jie-Min Prasad, Matthew Revert, and my classmates in LitReactor's Graphic Design 101 class, as well, for providing invaluable design suggestions during the process.

Finally, this has been a trying time for everyone, but I'm so glad that you —yes, you—made it through. For all of you who kept your distance, wore a mask, helped others when and how you could, and just kept going even when things seemed hopeless, you're amazing. I can't wait to see you again in person.

ABOUT THE AUTHOR

Gordon B. White is the author of the horror/weird fiction collection *As Summer's Mask Slips and Other Disruptions*, as well as the novellas *Rookfield* and *In Her Smile, the World* (with Rebecca J. Allred, 2022). A graduate of the Clarion West Writers Workshop, Gordon's stories have appeared in dozens of venues, including *Nightmare, Pseudopod, The Best Horror of the Year Vol. 12*, and the Bram Stoker Award® winning anthology *Borderlands 6*. He regularly contributes reviews and interviews to outlets such as *Nightmare, Lightspeed,* and *The Outer Dark* podcast. You can find him online at www.gordonb-white.com.